A greedy _____ _____ wormed its way across Ruben Hatch's ugly mouth. "Wait'll the rest of the gang hears this," he said excitedly. "Twenty thousand!"

"Twenty thousand?" echoed both Stenger and Gentry.

Hatch held up the letter so both men could read it. His partners swore with elation.

"You won't forget my share, will you?" asked Owens, an avaricious glint in his eyes.

Ruben Hatch cast a furtive glance at his two men, then looked at the skinny Wells Fargo agent and said, "Forget your share, Wally? Of course not." Reaching under his sheepskin coat and pulling a long-bladed hunting knife from its sheath, he added, "You're gonna get your share right now."

When Owens saw the deadly blade, he leapt backward, whirled, and went for his desk. His eyes were wild as Hatch drove the knife full-haft into the little man's back. Though Owens was arching in pain, he was still able to open the drawer and lift out a small-caliber revolver. . . .

The Badge Series
Ask your bookseller for the books you have missed

THE BADGE: BOOK 5

★

LONDON'S REVENGE

★

Bill Reno

 Created by the producers of
Stagecoach, Wagons West,
White Indian, and Winning
the West.

Book Creations Inc., Canaan, NY · Lyle Kenyon Engel, Founder

BANTAM BOOKS
TORONTO · NEW YORK · LONDON · SYDNEY · AUCKLAND

LONDON'S REVENGE

*A Bantam Book / published by arrangement with
Book Creations, Inc.*

Bantam edition / June 1988

*Produced by Book Creations, Inc.
Lyle Kenyon Engel: Founder*

ISBN 0-553-27217-9

Published simultaneously in the United States and Canada

*Bantam Books are published by Bantam Books, a division of Ban-
tam Doubleday Dell Publishing Group, Inc. Its trademark, consist-
ing of the words "Bantam Books" and the portrayal of a rooster, is
Registered in U.S. Patent and Trademark Office and in other
countries. Marca Registrada. Bantam Books, 666 Fifth Avenue,
New York, New York 10103.*

PRINTED IN THE UNITED STATES OF AMERICA

O   0 9 8 7 6 5 4 3 2 1

LONDON'S
REVENGE

American Indians fashioned
bows of hickory, mesquite, and
other hard wood, though occasionally
they used sections of bone or cow's horn,
held together with sinew. Arrowheads were
created by chipping flint into the proper shape
with a pointed piece of bone or a stone hammer.
While most quivers were made of tanned cow or
buffalo hide, sometimes the skin of a beaver, otter,
coyote, mountain lion, or black bear was used, often
with the fur left intact.

R. TOELKE '87

Prologue

The raw wind seemed to howl with savage pleasure as it knifed through the cracks around the door of the old abandoned cabin. Sheriff Matthew London ripped the last leg from the ancient oak table and carefully laid it on the fire that was crackling in the dusty stone fireplace. What was left of the table would keep the fire going for another hour, he figured.

London winced as he limped to the frosted window, his injured leg throbbing with pain. Rubbing a spot of glass clear with his elbow, he peered out into the snow-covered, windswept Montana plains. Looking westward, the sheriff of Yellowstone County wished there was some way to eliminate the miles between this one-room cabin and his office in Billings, where there was plenty of firewood stored. But he was stuck here in this cold, dreary cabin, and he had to manage as best he could until this whole drama had played itself out.

He pictured his deputy, Will Baker, who had just turned twenty-seven, and old Dusty Canfield sitting next to the potbellied stove, comfortable and toasty. Dusty was probably spinning one of his yarns about how rough things were in the *old* West. Matt London could almost hear the seasoned veteran talk about how Montana used to be twice as snowy and three times colder than it was now in the last weeks of 1890. In spite of his pain Matt London smiled, thinking of the crusty old man. Dusty was a true

1

friend, and London was glad he had not been a victim of the brutal Van Horns, the family responsible for the bullet in his own leg.

London limped across the earthen floor and looked down at Hale Van Horn, handcuffed to the post that held up the roof. The outlaw was beginning to stir. He had been knocked out cold when London hit him—hard enough to jar his ancestry three generations back.

Hauling himself over to the window on the east side of the cabin, the sheriff scraped it as clear of frost as possible and gazed out. The glaring snow had a wind-worn, glazed look. Even with the sun at its highest peak, the temperature outside was a good twenty below; when night came, it would get even colder.

There was nothing moving on the plains, no sign of the Van Horn brothers—yet. But they would come as sure as Monday follows Sunday—Ben and Clete Van Horn, with Jimmy, their younger brother, leading them. They would have no trouble tracking London and their oldest brother to the old cabin; the trail left in the snow would lead the Van Horns straight to it. London had left plenty of blood in the snow as well.

Turning to lean against the wall, the sheriff loosened the belt on his blood-soaked pantleg. He had strapped the belt around his thigh just above the spot where Jimmy Van Horn's bullet had ripped into him. He had been releasing the belt for a few minutes every quarter hour to ward off gangrene. *A lot of difference it's going to make,* he thought ruefully.

Matt London knew there was no way he could hold off the Van Horns. He had no rifle. His Colt .45 was empty in its holster. His horse lay dead in the snow a quarter mile to the east. And with his wounded leg he could not go anywhere.

He waited another minute and then tightened the leather tourniquet again. He sighed and looked out the window, seeing nothing more in the snow. He wondered how much longer it would take the Van Horns to reach the cabin. With no fire he and Hale Van Horn would not last more than a few hours. *The big question is,* he thought, *will the Van Horns have the pleasure of torturing and killing me, or will they find me frozen to death?*

His attention was drawn to Hale, who was slowly shaking his head. It would take the man a few more minutes to clear his brain.

Sliding down the wall to a sitting position, Sheriff Matthew London pondered the series of events that had brought him to this final day in his thirty-three years of life. It had all begun three weeks before, early in the last week in November. . . .

Chapter One

The Montana plains had endured countless centuries of ravaging winters, and the icy wind that rammed full force against the three riders carried the promise of another one. Fresh glistening snow mantled the rolling land, and the pale November sunlight shafted through high drifting clouds.

Turtling their necks into the pulled-up collars of the sheepskin coats they wore, outlaws Ruben Hatch, Gene Stenger, and Nolan Gentry bent their heads against the merciless wind as Billings came into view to the west. The misty vapor that came from Gentry's mouth was whipped away by the wind as he said to Ruben Hatch, "Boss, what if there's a customer in the Wells Fargo office when we go in? We can't wait around forever, but we sure can't let Wally tell us the news about the payroll in front of anybody."

Turning his freckled face toward Gentry, the redheaded outlaw leader replied, "We don't have to talk. Wally's got it all down on paper. He'll hand me an envelope, and the paper will be in it. After we warm up a little, we'll slip on out."

"You mean, if there's somebody else in the office," put in Gene Stenger.

"Yeah." Hatch nodded. "If Owens is alone, we'll go ahead and kill him right then."

"You sure you want him dead, boss?" asked Nolan Gentry. "I mean, he might be of use to us again sometime."

4

"If this payroll is as big as he's led me to believe," said Hatch, "we won't be needin' him anymore. That way, if the law somehow traces the leak back to Wally Owens, he won't be able to blab about who he gave the information to. No sense takin' a chance on it. Owens dies, if not while we're in the office, then just as soon as he *is* alone. And remember, boys, no guns. We use a knife. I ain't hankerin' to mess with that show-off of a sheriff."

Gene Stenger chuckled dryly. "Ain't nobody in his right mind gonna go up against Matt London."

Billings, Montana, lay in winter's grip with deep snow-drifts piled against buildings large and small. The uneven, snow-covered rooflines lay stark against the cold blue sky. A few people moved about on Main Street as the three riders hauled up in front of the Wells Fargo office. Wind-driven snow followed them through the door as they entered. They were pleased to find Fargo agent Wally Owens alone.

Owens, a small, thin man in his early fifties, resembled a skeleton that seemed unable to shed its skin. Rising from behind his desk as the three men came in, he smiled and said, "All set, Ruben."

"Good!" exclaimed Hatch as the slight man handed him a brown envelope. The flap was folded down but not sealed.

"Since we're alone," Owens said, grinning, "take a look at it."

Hatch pulled out the enclosed sheet of paper, unfolded it, and read it silently:

Ruben—
The information just came through on the wire. The Army payroll is being shipped from back East and will be on the stage that arrives in Billings from Miles City on December 1. There will be two guards on the stage, posing as businessmen. They will be well-armed since the payroll is $20,000. The stage is due in Billings at two o'clock in the afternoon that

day. Army troops will be here to pick it up for
distribution to forts Belknap, Harrison, and Fetterman.
Don't forget to drop off my share.

                                        Wally

A greedy smile wormed its way across Ruben Hatch's
ugly mouth. "Wait'll the rest of the gang hears this," he
said excitedly. "Twenty thousand!"

"Twenty thousand?" echoed both Stenger and Gentry.

Hatch held it up so both men could read it. As he
stuffed it back in the envelope and sealed it, his partners
swore with elation, Gentry adding, "December first—hey,
that's just a week from today!"

"You won't forget my share, will you?" asked Owens, an
avaricious glint in his eyes.

Ruben Hatch cast a furtive glance at his two men, then
looked at the skinny agent and said, "Forget your share,
Wally? Of course not." Reaching under his sheepskin coat
and pulling a long-bladed hunting knife from its sheath, he
added, "You're gonna get your share right now."

When Owens saw the deadly blade, he leaped backward, whirled, and went for his desk. His eyes were wild
as Hatch drove the knife full-haft into the little man's
back. Though Owens was arching in pain, he was still able
to open the drawer and lift out a small-caliber revolver.
Hatch jerked the knife out and was moving closer to stab
Owens again, but the wiry agent was bringing the gun into
play.

Nolan Gentry, seeing the danger his boss was in, quickly
drew his gun and fired, hitting Wally Owens in the chest.
Owens gasped and staggered backward, bumping up against
his desk and hanging there for a moment like a puppet on
a string. Then he fell dead.

"Sorry for using the gun, boss," breathed Gentry, "but
he'd have shot you if I hadn't."

"You did right," Hatch said, stuffing the brown envelope into a coat pocket. "C'mon. Let's get out of here!"

                    *   *   *

At the same time that the three outlaws were entering the stage office to see Fargo agent Wally Owens, Deputy Will Baker looked up from where he sat at the desk in the sheriff's office and saw a tall shadow silhouetted against the opaque glass door. It was Sheriff Matt London, pausing to speak with someone on the boardwalk before entering.

Baker studied the shadow of his boss, who was his hero in every sense of the word. The deputy was pleased to be London's right-hand man, and he knew that he would lay down his life for London if he were ever called upon to do it.

It also pleased Baker that he had a build similar to his hero's. London stood six four in his bare feet and weighed a sinewy one hundred and ninety-five pounds. Baker was an inch shorter and seven pounds lighter, close enough to allow the deputy a touch of pride.

Will Baker's goal was to emulate the sheriff in every way that he could. London, tough as steel and fast as lightning with the iron on his hip, had a reputation for being rough with outlaws and never letting them intimidate him. The deputy was determined to follow his boss's example.

Cold air gusted into the room as Matt London opened the door and stepped in. Shutting the door, he moved to the potbellied stove, pulled off his gloves, and held his palms toward the heat. He turned his chocolate-brown eyes toward his deputy and said, "I think winter's coming."

"I would say so." Baker grinned. "Why don't you take your coat off and stay awhile?"

"I will as soon as I thaw out my fingers," London replied, flexing them and then rubbing his hands together over the rising heat. "Dusty still around?"

"Uh . . . no." The deputy grinned. "He's across the street, getting some uh . . . medicine."

The ruggedly handsome sheriff arched his eyebrows. "Medicine? Across the street? Doc's office isn't across the street."

Chortling, Baker said, "According to Dusty, the saloon sells medicine too."

London laughed, then asked, "Anything important in the mail? I saw the Sheridan stagecoach arrive a while ago."

Sifting through some papers on top of the desk, Baker replied, "One letter here you ought to know about. Here it is. From the Sheridan County sheriff down in Wyoming."

"Sam Courtney?"

"Yeah. Wants you to know that he has good reason to believe Ruben Hatch and his gang may be headed for these parts."

"Hatch, huh? We've got posters on him from Wyoming, but I haven't heard of his operating in Montana before. Courtney say what his good reason is?"

"Nope."

"Well, if Sam Courtney says he has a good reason for something, I'll take his word for it. Man's a first-rate lawman."

"Oh, he's okay, I guess," said Baker, lacing his fingers behind his head and leaning back in the chair. "But he can't hold a candle to you."

Peeling off his heavy sheepskin coat, London snickered. "Will, my boy, don't you think you've got me just a little too high on your hero list?"

"List?" echoed the deputy. "There have to be at least *two* to have a list. Far as I'm concerned, you're alone in your class."

Shaking his head as he hung the coat on a corner rack, London said, "Son, I hope it's not going to be a big letdown to you when one of these days you find out I'm made of mortal flesh just like everybody else." Removing his hat and placing it over his coat, he added, "Someday, when you're wear—"

London's words were cut short by the sound of a gunshot. Baker jumped out of his chair as the sheriff headed for the door, saying, "It was muffled. Came from inside a building."

With his deputy on his heels London bolted out into the icy air. Both men were looking from the left to the right when they saw three figures suddenly dash out of the Wells Fargo office some seventy yards to the north. Whipping out his gun, the sheriff shouted, "Hold it right there!"

One of the fleeing men already had a gun in his hand. While the other two were leaping into their saddles, he sent two shots at the lawman. One of the bullets hummed past Will Baker's head, causing him to slip and fall in the snow. London drew a quick bead and dropped the man before he could fit a boot into his stirrup. Dogging back the hammer and firing at the other two, who were now galloping away, London knocked the closest one from his saddle.

The third man was getting away. London fired again and heard him yelp, but his horse was quickly carrying him beyond pistol range. The sheriff took one more shot, but he knew there was no way he could hit the man now. The injured man's horse turned east and disappeared.

London ran toward the two men he had shot down, looking back at Will Baker, who was once again on his feet and following. The first man London had shot was dead. Baker drew up and paused, looking down at the dead man while the sheriff moved on to the other one. Seeing that the second man was still breathing, London knelt down beside him. He recognized him immediately from the wanted posters in his office.

When the mortally wounded outlaw opened his eyes and seemed to focus them on the sheriff, London said, "You're Gene Stenger, aren't you?"

The dying man only looked at him. At that moment Will Baker walked up and said, "Matt, the dead one is Nolan Gentry. One of Ruben Hatch's gang. We've got a poster on him."

"This one's a Hatch man too," London said evenly. "Gene Stenger." Turning back to the wounded man, he asked, "Was the other one Hatch himself?"

"Looked like him to me, Matt," spoke up Baker. "Distance was too great to be positive, but I think it was Hatch. Sheriff Courtney's information was right."

Stenger gasped, coughed, and went limp. "He's dead, Will," said London. "Let's check the Fargo office."

Three miles northeast of Billings, Barth Van Horn and his three oldest sons were riding home from town. While the bitter wind clawed at their heavy coats and plucked at their broad-brimmed hats, they discussed the financial plight that had fallen upon them. While never having been a wealthy man, Barth and his large family had once managed to make a comfortable living from farming his land, which bordered the Crow Indian reservation and was east and north of Billings. It was when the federal government had forced him to sell a good third of his acreage for the Crow reservation for a pittance that things had begun a slow decline at the Van Horn farm. He had sunk what money there was into improving the farm and then had overextended himself by buying livestock on credit. But the animals had died of disease during a bad winter two years back, and now the creditors were pressing for their ten thousand dollars and threatening to take the farm if the money was not paid.

Hale Van Horn, at twenty-nine the oldest son, pulled his hat tight against the wind and said, "Pa, I told you we were makin' this ride for nothin'. I knew those bankers wouldn't loan us the money."

"We had to try, Hale," responded the old man, working his huge arms against the cold. Barth Van Horn was a beefy Dutchman with a florid face that made him look perpetually sunburned. Though he was sixty and what hair he had left had turned silver, he was still as strong as a bull. He stood six feet four inches in height and tipped the scales at two hundred thirty pounds. Hale was about the same size, as were twenty-seven-year-old Wes and his brother Clete, who was two years younger.

Wes spoke up and said, "How were we to know Mr. Garvin and Mr. Carney wouldn't loan us the money? Our place is worth plenty more than ten thousand dollars."

"Yeah?" Hale replied. "Then how come Garvin said he wouldn't even loan us a thousand, let alone ten thousand? Who's he to call us a bad risk?"

"Maybe if you hadn't gotten so hot under the collar and called him that name he'd have changed his mind," Wes countered.

Hale's face tinted. His pale blue eyes flashed as he snapped, "Watch your mouth, little brother."

"Knock it off, boys," their father said calmly, then suddenly he raised his hand and turned in the saddle, as if having heard something. "What's that?"

Van Horn's three oldest sons quickly turned and followed his line of sight as a horse and rider came into view on the road behind them. The man was slumped in the saddle, but he saw the Van Horns and pulled back on the reins, bringing the horse to a shuddering halt that caused him to slide from the saddle and collapse in a heap in the snow.

As the Van Horns turned their horses and rode closer, they saw that the man was bleeding, staining the snow red. He was breathing hard, and plumes of hazy vapor came from his mouth and were quickly dissipated by the cutting wind. As the four men dismounted, the senior Van Horn said, "Looks like you took a bullet, my friend."

"Yeah," breathed the redheaded man shakily. "Had a little dispute at one of the saloons in town. Other guy came out of it better than I did."

Barth Van Horn bent close to see the bullet hole in the man's coat. "I'd say he shot you in the back."

"I . . . I need your help," he said weakly.

"We'd better get him to the doctor in town," spoke up Wes.

"No!" the man gasped. "No doctor . . . please. Do, uh . . . do you have womenfolk at home? One of them could maybe dig out the slug and patch me up."

When the four Van Horns looked as though they were about to deny him his request, the redheaded man said hastily, "Look, I'll pay you. I'll pay you well. I need another favor too."

"What's that?" Barth Van Horn asked.

The wounded man pulled a sealed brown envelope from his coat pocket and told Van Horn that he needed it delivered to some friends of his near Bighorn, some fifty miles to the northeast. He would draw the four men a map so they could find the place. If they would take him to their home and get him patched up, he would write a note to his friends telling them to pay the bearer of the envelope five hundred dollars upon delivery.

The mention of five hundred dollars set up a light in Barth Van Horn's pale blue eyes. Looking around at his sons, he said, "Sure, mister. You bet we'll help you. I see you're gettin' some blood on the envelope. Want me to take it now?"

The redheaded man nodded, handing it to Van Horn. Ruben Hatch was relieved that his men would get word of the payroll shipment. He was in no shape to deliver it himself. He had taken Matt London's bullet in his left shoulder and had barely made it three miles from Billings before falling from his horse.

Barth Van Horn glanced at the envelope briefly and then stuck it in a coat pocket as he said, "Okay, boys, we need to get our friend here to the house. Holly and Sandra can fix him up."

The three brothers were about to hoist Ruben Hatch into his saddle when their father, looking off toward town, said, "Somebody's comin'."

"Yeah," said Hale. "A whole bunch of somebodies."

"Maybe I'm wrong, Pa," remarked Clete, tightening his hat against the pull of the bitter wind, "but the horse in the lead sure looks like the sheriff's. I'd say what we got comin' is a posse."

Barth looked down at the wounded man and said, "What did you say your name was, friend?"

The sullen outlaw remained silent, clutching at his

wounded shoulder and swearing under his breath as he
sank to his knees.

The posse drew up with their mounts scattering snow
and sending up clouds of vapor from their nostrils. Sheriff
Matt London ran his gaze over the Van Horns, dropped it
to Ruben Hatch, then looked at the older man and said,
"You and your boys stop him, Barth?"

The senior Van Horn was certain now that he had come
upon some kind of an outlaw. If so, there was probably a
reward on the man's head, he figured. Knowing the tracks
in the snow would tell the true story, Van Horn replied,
"He just rode up to us, Sheriff. He ain't told us who he is,
but me and the boys figured him to be a wanted man, so
we were about to saddle him up and bring him to you. Is
there a bounty on him?"

"I know there is in Wyoming," London said. "Not sure
about Montana. But I'll check on it. You were just about
to bring me *Ruben Hatch.*"

The Van Horns were stunned. They knew the name;
Hatch was a notorious outlaw.

Ruben Hatch's face grew mottled with anger as he
growled through clenched teeth, "He's lyin', Sheriff. They
were gonna help me escape!"

Feigning innocence, Barth Van Horn looked surprised
as he said to London, *"He's* the one who's lyin', Sheriff.
We didn't even know he was Hatch! Why should we help
him escape?"

Barth Van Horn's eyes met Hatch's as the outlaw's face
grew darker. Van Horn had been gambling that the brown
envelope Hatch had given him contained something the
outlaw did not want the sheriff to see. When Hatch failed
to mention the envelope, Van Horn knew he was right.

Matt London looked at Hatch and said, "I'll get you to
the doctor in Billings first, Hatch. The murder charges for
the death of Wally Owens can wait till later."

Within minutes London and the posse had Hatch in
their custody and were riding away slowly, heading for
town. As they rode off, London heard Barth Van Horn call

out, "You check into that reward money, Sheriff! We'll be in town in a few days to see about it."

London waved, nodded, and turned his attention to Ruben Hatch, who was doubled over in his saddle.

When the posse was out of hearing range, Barth Van Horn pulled the envelope from his coat pocket and said, "Well, boys, since we ain't gonna get paid to deliver this, we might as well see what it's about."

Hale, Wes, and Clete stomped their feet and swung their arms to keep their blood circulating while Barth ripped open the envelope and took out the sheet of paper. As his eyes took in the words, they widened. Then he grinned broadly and exclaimed, "Boys, we don't need no stinkin' loan. In fact we're never gonna have to plow another field again. If what I'm thinkin' works out, we're gonna be rich!"

"What are you talkin' about, Pa?" Hale demanded.

"Here," said the old man, jamming the paper into Hale's gloved hand. "Read it out loud to your brothers."

When Hale had finished, six wide eyes were fixed on the elder Van Horn as Wes said, "What's this got to do with us gettin' rich, Pa?"

Van Horn laughed, beating his cold hands together. "Come on, Wes! You weren't born yesterday! If Ruben Hatch can rob the stagecoach of twenty thousand dollars, why can't we?"

There was a quavery edge to Wes's voice as he protested, "I'll tell you why, Pa. Because we ain't outlaws! We ain't never done anything like that before. Sure, we've rustled a few head of cattle lately since things have been thin . . . and Hale once took a fifty-dollar bill out of old man Murray's cash box when he wasn't lookin', but a stagecoach robbery?"

"Yeah, Pa," Clete interjected. "We're not outlaws like Ruben Hatch and his gang."

"For twenty thousand dollars we can *become* outlaws,"

Hale stated. "I'm with you, Pa. Livin' straight and narrow ain't got us nowhere. Might be better bein' an outlaw."

"If it works, we'll be a *rich* bunch of outlaws, boys!" Van Horn said excitedly.

"I don't like it, Pa," snapped Clete. "And Ma's not gonna like it either, not to mention Holly and Sandra."

"Who's boss in this family, Clete?" grumbled the silver-haired man. "Me or the women?"

"You are, Pa."

"Then we'll do what I say. Just think of it! We won't have to kowtow to those bankers and we won't lose the farm. I'll guarantee you that Ma and the girls will be plenty glad to have ample food on the table again . . . some new clothes too."

"But what about the bounty money?" Wes asked. "Maybe that'll be enough—"

"We'll be lucky if it amounts to a thousand," Barth cut in. "Now, don't be goin' soft on me, boy. It'll be easy. Hell, they'll think it was Hatch's gang that done it. No one'll ever suspect us."

"Let's go home and tell the others the good news, Pa," Hale said. "We've got to make plans too. We've only got a week to get ready for this."

Chapter Two

On the morning of December 1, 1890, Sheriff Matt London made his way along the snow-covered main street of Billings, heading for his office. The air was frigid, but there was only a slight breeze. The relative calm was in sharp contrast with the blustery storm of the previous day. The Montana sky was cold and clear, the heatless sun just putting in an appearance on the eastern horizon.

London bid good morning to the only two people he saw on the street, and he entered his office. Will Baker was just closing the iron door on the potbellied stove. The blazing wood in the stove was giving off desultory popping sounds.

"Morning, Will," said the tall man, closing the door behind him. "Whew! It's cold out there!"

"Thermometer in front of Doc's office says twenty-six below, boss," said Baker.

"Dusty in yet?"

"Yeah. He's stoking the fire back in the cellblock so Ruben Hatch doesn't freeze to death. I think Hatch is trying to coerce the old guy into letting him out."

London chuckled. "Ruben might as well talk to a tree stump."

Shedding his sheepskin coat and hat, the sheriff ran his fingers through his mop of curly black hair. He looked toward the rear of the building as banging noises came from the cellblock. London knew how much Dusty disliked Ruben Hatch. Ever since the outlaw was brought in a week ago, he and Dusty had been at each other. Hatch had stood trial this past week and had been sentenced to hang, but Dusty had made it clear that he would just as soon see the outlaw freeze to death in the meantime.

In the six years that Matt London had been sheriff of Yellowstone County, he had come to rely on Dusty Canfield. The old man had once been a deputy town marshal, but when the hardships of old age left him unemployed, he had looked for work wherever he could—and a stint of guard duty at a jail, where there was warmth and good company, was always his preference. When London had first come to Yellowstone County as its sheriff, Dusty had been quick to welcome him to the area, and soon the old-timer had made himself a fixture in the sheriff's office.

Dusty Canfield's uneven footsteps echoed from the cell-block at the rear of the jail. Then the door opened, exposing a weathered old face under a hat that looked as though a horse had stepped on its crown and a packrat had chewed on the brim. Dusty walked into the room with his usual limp, which had been caused by a bullet shattering a bone in his left leg some forty years earlier.

The old man looked the sheriff up and down and said in a cranky tone, "I don't know how come you attract criminals like that jackass back there, Matthew."

"What's he done now?" asked London.

Dusty limped over to a tarnished brass cuspidor in the corner of the room and spit a brown stream of tobacco juice. "He can't stand a little cool air. He's always wantin' me to stoke the fire in the stove for him. Far as I'm concerned, he can freeze to death. Besides that, he keeps tryin' to bribe me to help him escape. Started out sayin' he'd pay me a hundred dollars, and now he's upped the offer to five hundred. I'm thinkin' seriously of takin' him up on it."

Will Baker laughed. "I'm surprised you haven't done it already, you old goat. Five hundred dollars would sure buy a lot of that Bull Durham tobacco you chew."

Dusty Canfield's wrinkled skin was the color of mahogany, especially ruddy around the cheekbones. Straggly locks of white hair protruded from under his dirty old hat, and the bottom half of his craggy face was clouded with white stubble. He smiled at the deputy, revealing a large gap where two upper teeth had been. His hazel eyes glinted as he retorted, "You're half right, Will. All I need money for is the Durham. With you around there's already plenty of *bull!*" The husky voice sounded as though it had been strained by years of shouting against the wind.

While the deputy mumbled something to himself, Dusty looked at Matt London, who was laughing. "Let's get serious a minute, Matthew. Do you think Ruben Hatch's gang will try to spring him before the hangin'?"

"I expect them to try to do just that," the handsome sheriff said, nodding. "Killers like Ruben Hatch don't die easy."

Dusty looked at the large calendar on the wall behind Will Baker's desk. Squinting, he said, "What's he got, four days left?"

"Yes," said London. "Four days. His gang could show up at any time, but they'll most likely try to spring him when we take him out to hang. We can't be sure that they won't try before, though."

Dusty limped to his double-barreled shotgun, which was propped against the wall. Picking it up, he said, "If you would like, Matthew, I'll just camp right here in the office till the hangin's over." Patting the long, shiny barrels, he added, "If them outlaws show up, Fanny May here will blast 'em to kingdom come."

Baker laughed. "Dusty, do you name everything you own? You call that old shack of yours Mary Alice, and the tree in your front yard is Lily Pearl. Your old mule is Uncle Amos, and your shotgun is Fanny May! Tell me, what do you call your hat?"

With a big grin on his face Dusty swept the mangled felt hat from his head and said, "I call it *beautiful!*"

Both lawmen laughed, and then Matt London said, "I'll

take you up on your offer, Dusty. You camp here in the office until Ruben Hatch goes to meet his maker. That will give Will and me a little more liberty to move about town."

The old man's eyes twinkled with delight. "That'll be just dandy with me. 'Course, my meals will be provided by the county while I'm on guard duty, right?"

Sheriff London grinned and nodded his head. "Yes, you old panhandler. Yellowstone County will fill your belly while you guard the place."

Dusty limped to the spittoon in the corner and spit in it again. "Gotta hand it to you, Matthew," he cackled. "You know how to pick your hired help." Then casting a sly look at Will Baker, he added, "Well, I guess you're allowed *one* mistake!"

When Baker wadded up a piece of paper and threw it at the old man, bouncing it off his head, Dusty cackled again. "You're a good shot with that, Will. It's too bad you can't hit the mark with that little gal you're head over heels about!"

Baker arched his eyebrows.

"You know what I mean. I'm talkin' about your droolin' every time you get around that Holly Van Horn."

Will Baker's face tinted.

Dusty guffawed and, pointing at the sheriff, said to him, "Lookee there, Matthew. I done struck the nail right smack on the head. Your poor ugly deputy has it bad for the little blonde with the big blue eyes, but she won't even let him court her!"

Matt London ran his gaze across the handsome features of his young deputy. Will Baker had black wavy hair, deep blue eyes, and a face that drew the attention of young women everywhere he went. London could never figure out why Will Baker let Dusty's teasing about being ugly get under his skin.

Baker was indeed fuming as he said, "Look, you old geezer, I asked Holly to go to the barn dance last week, and she said she wanted to go with me, but her father wouldn't let her."

"Aw, she was just bein' kind," said the old man, and soon his laughter was joined by the sheriff's.

"Okay, you two," Baker said, rising from the desk chair. "Just keep laughing. But remember my words: One of these days I'll be courting Holly. You'll see."

"I bet you won't," Dusty said.

Walking around the desk to where the old man was standing, Baker said, "Put your money where your mouth is, friend. How much do you want to bet?"

Baker knew that Dusty was less willing than most people to part with his money, and he was therefore somewhat surprised when the old man reached for his jacket, pulled out a well-worn wallet, and produced a large paper bill. Shaking it in Baker's face, he said, "Here's five dollars that says you'll never stand a chance of courting Holly Van Horn."

The deputy pulled a matching bill from his pocket and retorted, "This one says I will."

"You've got three months," Dusty replied. "Then I'm calling in the bet."

"You're on," Baker said, grinning.

Looking at the sheriff, the old man said, "Matthew, you hold the money."

Accepting both bills, London asked Baker, "Isn't Holly of age? How can Barth keep her from going to the barn dance with you?"

"She's twenty-two," Baker replied. "But she lives under her father's roof, and he rules with an iron hand."

"Why doesn't she leave home?" asked Dusty.

"Because of her mother," the deputy answered. "Myrtle Van Horn has a bad heart, and Holly feels an obligation to stay close and take care of her."

"Seems I heard that Clete has a wife livin' with him out there," said Dusty. "Couldn't she be the one to take care of Mrs. Van Horn?"

"Clete does have a wife—Sandra, I think her name is," Baker said, nodding.

"Don't think I've ever seen her," said London.

"Holly says she's never been to town," the deputy answered. "She stays on the place all the time. But with Sandra being just an in-law and not a blood relation, Holly feels that the responsibility of caring for her mother is strictly hers."

"She's to be commended," Dusty said, heading for the cuspidor again.

The deputy sighed. "I wish Holly's family were different. Getting to know her better wouldn't be so hard then."

"Barth Van Horn and his sons are pesky and troublesome. Especially since the Crows got part of their land."

"They've sure gotten clannish," put in Dusty, spitting again. "They don't want to socialize with nobody no more. Seems like they're always wearin' chips on their shoulders."

"And lately they've been treading the line between lawful and unlawful behavior," London said. "Holly sure doesn't fit in with them."

"Holly is different because of her mother," Baker said. "She and her mother aren't happy about the ways of the Van Horn men, but there's nothing they can do. Barth's influence over his sons is too powerful."

"He is the big bull of the family, all right," said London. "But you'd think at least one or two of those boys—"

Dusty Canfield, who was looking out the office window, interrupted, "Well, speak of the devil!"

Matt London stepped to the window, his deputy following him. Outside Barth Van Horn and his three oldest sons were dismounting in front of the office.

"Wonder what they want," Baker said.

"Probably want to know about the reward money," mused London.

Heavy boots thumped and scraped on the boardwalk, and then the door burst open to reveal the huge bulk of

Barth Van Horn, followed by Hale, Wes, and Clete. A blast of cold air came with them.

Will Baker had noted before that with one exception all of the Van Horn sons were big and beefy like their father. Jimmy, only sixteen, was still just lanky. Holly, who was slender and petite, was the only child to favor her mother.

Wes Van Horn kicked the door shut. With the entry of the four big men the sheriff's office seemed to diminish in size.

"We're here about the reward money," grunted Barth, his usually florid face even brighter red because of the cold.

Standing as tall as the Van Horns, Matt London responded quickly, "Sorry, Barth, there isn't any."

The old man's ruddy face took on a harsh look. "What are you talkin' about? We gave you that outlaw. We got it comin' to us."

Squaring his wide shoulders, London said crisply, "There's no reward money being offered on Ruben Hatch in Montana, Barth. In Wyoming he's got two thousand on his head. But he's not in Wyoming. He's here. He was tried here, and he was convicted of murder here. He's going to hang here. Like I said, I'm sorry, but you won't be getting any reward money."

Hale Van Horn stepped in front of the sheriff, his pale blue eyes flashing as he barked, "There's reward money, all right, London. Only it's *you* who's gonna get it. You're lyin' to us so you can stuff your own pockets!"

Will Baker tensed, and Dusty Canfield quickly set his gaze on Matt London's face.

Holding his temper, the sheriff spoke coolly to Hale. "I'm going to try to forget you said that."

"No, you remember it, London!" Hale blared. "All you tin stars are dirty dealers! My pa's brother was killed because of an underhanded greedy lawman a few years ago. We Van Horns haven't had any use for your kind ever since. And here we are bein' *robbed* by another lawman!"

Matt London's dark-brown eyes took on an arctic chill.

With gritty contempt in his voice he rasped, "If that's what you want to think, you go ahead, Hale. But I don't want to hear it anymore. Open your mouth about it again and I'll shut it for you. And when I do, you'll be looking at the world through those bars back there!"

Hale Van Horn rolled his massive shoulders as he hissed, "Just take off that badge, mister lawman, and we'll see just how tough you really are!"

Barth Van Horn laid a firm hand on his oldest son's shoulder. "That's enough, Hale. Even if you whipped him, we still wouldn't get the money that's comin' to us. This place is beginnin' to stink. Let's get out of here."

Hale burned the sheriff with hate-filled eyes as he grated, "Yeah, Pa. It *does* stink in here."

As the Van Horn sons turned toward the door, their father pointed a stiff finger at Will Baker and growled, "And you, Romeo! Stay away from my daughter!"

Will Baker stepped up to the huge man and said defensively, "Mr. Van Horn, I have always been a gentleman when talking to Holly. She'll tell you herself. The only move I made was to ask her to go to the barn dance with me last week."

Van Horn's face deepened in color. "You noticed she didn't go with you, didn't you?"

"Of course."

"Did she tell you why?"

"Yes, sir. She told me you wouldn't allow her to go with me."

"That's right!" the red-faced man blurted. "And now, I'll tell you myself. *You stay away from Holly!* My daughter knows she's not to be friendly with you or anybody who wears a badge. Why, you're all nothin' but hypocrites, hidin' behind your pieces of tin so you can bend the law to suit yourselves. I'm tellin' you once more, boy. Stay away from my daughter!"

Will Baker's self-control was beginning to crumble, and he pressed his lips together in an attempt to maintain it.

He remained silent, knowing that anything he had to say would be worse than saying nothing.

London cut the silence, stating sharply, "You've had your say, Barth. Now drag your carcass out of my office and take your pups with you!"

Van Horn's massive head whirled around, and London could see the blood vessels popping out on his face. The huge man seemed ready to snap at the sheriff, but he paused, as if recognizing the danger in London's sullen eyes. Van Horn seemed to know better than to push the sheriff any further. Someone might get hurt—and it would probably be a Van Horn.

The big man grunted and then turned, pushing his way past his sons and pulling open the door. As the cold air filled the room, he bowled his way outside, followed by Hale, Wes, and Clete. They did not bother to close the door.

Limping to the door, Dusty called the four men a few choice names under his breath and then pushed it shut. London looked at his deputy and said, "What are you going to do, Will?"

Will Baker took a deep breath and replied, "Holly's old enough to make her own decisions and to know who she wants as friends. Van Horn has no right to tell her who to see and not to see."

"It's a wonder he even lets her off the place," said Dusty. "I'm surprised he lets her enter the shootin' contest at the fair every year, what with all the men around."

Will Baker shook his head morosely. "It was at last year's fair that I first noticed Holly. I watched her outshoot every woman in the contest."

"She could probably outshoot every *man* in the county too," London said with a grin.

"Every man but you," Baker replied, an admiring tone in his voice. "Nobody can outshoot you."

London laid a hand on his deputy's shoulder. "I think you're just a little biased."

Dusty wiped tobacco juice from his mouth with his

sleeve before adding, "The men in this here county had just better pray that old Dusty don't enter next year's contest. They'd see some real shootin' if I did!"

London laughed. "They don't have a contest for shotguns, Dusty."

"What do you mean, shotguns? Just because you ain't never seen me handle a rifle don't mean that I can't handle one. Why, one time when I was huntin' grizzlies up in Canada, I—"

"Oh, no!" exclaimed Baker. "Here comes another tale about the great and mighty adventures of the great and mighty Dusty Canfield! I've got some record-keeping work to do."

"And so do I!" London said, hurrying to the desk. "No time to listen to stories right now."

The leather-faced old man mumbled to himself and went to the window, frosting it up with his breath.

The Van Horns, boiling mad over their loss of the reward money, were certain that Matt London was keeping it for himself. They needed little excuse to vent some of their anger.

"We got time for a quick visit to the saloon before we head out to rob that stagecoach, Pa," said Hale. "Maybe we can belt down a couple drinks to warm us up."

Big Barth chuckled humorlessly and mumbled something under his breath. After he and his three burly sons had untied their horses, he led them up the street toward the Big Sky Saloon.

As they moved along, Hale drew up beside his father and said, "Well, Pa, I guess you let those two tin stars know how we feel about their kind."

"Yeah, Pa," put in Wes from behind. "I thought for a moment London was gonna tie into you."

"I wish he'd tie into *me*," said Hale, half turning so his brother could hear him. "I'd have me some fun makin' mincemeat out of that two-bit sheriff. It'd be a pleasure to stuff that badge right down his throat."

Barth Van Horn cast a dry glance at his oldest son. "Don't be too quick to light into Matt London, Hale. He may not have a lot of meat on his bones, but he's plenty tough. A lot of men who are bigger than he is have learned that the hard way."

Hale lifted his hat and then dropped it back on his head. "Guess you ain't seen your favorite blue-eyed son in a scrap lately, Pa. I can handle anybody that comes along. Includin' the famous Sheriff Matthew London."

"Just remember what I said," warned Hale's father.

As the Van Horn men approached the saloon, they saw three Crow Indians sitting on the boardwalk near the door, dressed in heavy furs and talking among themselves.

"Stupid Crows ain't got no better sense than to sit out here in the cold," whispered Wes.

"Indians don't feel the cold," commented Hale. "You have to be human or animal to feel the cold. They ain't neither."

Clete stifled a laugh.

"Let's go in and warm our tonsils," Van Horn spoke up.

"Not before I have a little fun," Hale said, itching to vent his anger toward Matt London. "Watch this."

While Wes, Clete, and their father tied up the horses, Hale made a wide circle and stepped onto the boardwalk some ten yards down the street from where the Indians sat, unnoticed by them. As he passed in front of the first Indian, he deliberately stumbled against the man's feet, lurching forward and making a big production of it. Regaining his balance, he pointed a finger at the Indian and with eyes blazing said, "Hey, you dirty redskin! You just tripped me!"

People on the street paused to watch.

The Indian seemed to recognize Hale and glanced nervously at his friends. Then, speaking softly, he said to Hale, "Not my wish to cause you to fall. Sorry."

"Sorry?" grated Hale. "*Sorry?* Not near as sorry as you're gonna be." With that he lunged furiously at the Indian, sinking his fingers into the fur coat and jerking him to his feet. Hale cocked his free arm and smashed his victim hard in the face. The Indian's knees buckled. Instantly the two other Crows jumped Hale, tumbling him into the street.

Barth Van Horn watched with barely disguised glee as Wes and Clete went to their brother's aid. The first Indian seemed to regain his awareness of what was happening, and he piled into the melee. Within moments the three Indians and the three Van Horn brothers were rolling in the dirty snow of the street, their fists swinging. A crowd quickly gathered, and people started shouting.

Dusty Canfield was still at the window of the sheriff's office when he heard the ruckus from down the street. Rushing to the door, he pulled it open and stuck out his head.

"What is it, Dusty?" London asked from behind his desk.

"We got trouble, Matthew. The Van Horns are fighting with some Crows down at the Big Sky!"

Leaving Dusty to guard the jail, the two lawmen clapped on their hats and grabbed their coats, slipping into them as they ran down the street. They pushed their way through the encircling crowd to find the Van Horn brothers sitting on top of the Crows, pounding them senseless. Barth Van Horn stood nearby, impassively watching the fight. London turned to his deputy and said, "Let me handle this, Will. Don't step in unless it gets real rough."

The younger man nodded.

Moving into the circle, the sheriff shouted, "All right! That's enough!" When London shouted a second time, all three Van Horn brothers stopped swinging.

"Get off them," commanded London.

Wes and Clete obeyed immediately, and the two Indians they had been pummeling scrambled to their feet, wiping blood from their faces. But Hale Van Horn, his fists still balled and an obstinate look in his eyes, remained on top of the third Indian.

"I said get off him!" barked London.

A wicked sneer curled Hale's upper lip. "Make me," he said.

The insolent challenge was all Matt London needed. Stomping toward the man, he growled, "If that's the way you want it . . ."

Hale braced himself as London closed in, but he stubbornly held on to the Indian, pressing him to the ground. The Crow was spitting blood and coughing. The sheriff sank steely fingers into Hale's coat collar and yanked him off the Indian, causing the man's huge form to cartwheel into the snow. The sheriff then helped the bleeding Indian to his feet and assisted him to where his companions stood.

Moments later Hale stood up, charging toward the sheriff like a thundering bull, but the nimble lawman sidestepped out of his attacker's path, letting the bulky man crash into the hitch rail.

Hale grunted and fell backward. Looking as though London's stunt had infuriated him, he swore and stood up.

"There's nothing to fight about now, Hale," London said coolly. "You've already released the Indian."

Color flared in Hale's face. "You're gonna wish you hadn't forced me to," he grunted. Fury spewed from his mouth as he again charged the tall lawman, swinging a meaty fist that was meant to remove London's head. But the sheriff ducked it, driving a savage blow to Hale's midsection and punching the wind from him. When the big man buckled, London hammered him with a fist at the side of the head. Hale staggered, dropped to one knee, then bounced back up. There was murder in his ice-blue eyes as he bounded after London again.

The agile lawman took off his hat and tossed it to the crowd. Dodging Hale's fists, he battered the irate man's nose viciously. Hale shook his head and came at London again, this time attempting to wrestle his opponent, but London bent down, drove his shoulder into Hale's midsection, lifted him off the ground, and flipped him over his back.

Hale hit the frozen ground hard and lay there for a minute, looking stunned and surprised at London's strength. After a moment or two of sucking hard for air, he struggled to get to his feet. The sheriff waited, ready to finish him off.

Suddenly Clete Van Horn pushed his way through the crowd from behind London, but he stopped short at the sight of Will Baker's Colt aimed at his belt buckle. Wordlessly Baker pursed his lips and slowly shook his head. Clete walked backward, dissolving into the crowd.

As Barth and Wes Van Horn stood side by side and watched what was happening, they gave each other a helpless look. Hale had bitten off more than he could chew, and now he was going to suffer the consequences. *I warned him,* Van Horn said to himself.

Hale lunged in desperation at the sheriff, swinging wildly with both fists, but London abruptly stopped him with a merciless blow to the jaw. As Hale's head reeled, London's other fist caught it on the rebound. Hale's legs began to buckle. When London gave him a sharp blow to the back of the neck, Hale went down hard, his face smashing into the dirty snow.

Standing over Hale Van Horn, Matt London looked down at him as the big man slowly raised himself up on an elbow, his breath rasping. Then his eyes rolled back in his head, and he dropped flat, unconscious.

There were subdued cheers from the townspeople, who had little liking for the Van Horns.

London took his hat from a friendly bystander. Dropping it over his curly hair, he shot a cold glance at Barth Van Horn. "Take your sons home, Barth. I don't want any more trouble from your clan in this town."

Van Horn squared his shoulders and retorted, "Those stinkin' Crows started it!"

Without comment the sheriff moved to where the three Indians stood and talked to them in quiet tones. No one else could hear what he was saying, but the Crows shook their heads in obvious disagreement. London spoke some more, and then the Indians nodded and moved away, heading for their horses. London turned, stepped over to the senior Van Horn, and said flatly, "The Crows are leaving peaceably—but they say you're a liar."

Van Horn bristled at London's words. "And you'll believe those filthy savages before you will a white man!"

"You're wrong on two counts and correct on one," the sheriff said blandly. "The Crows are not filthy, they are not savages, and I *do* believe them."

Van Horn swore and spit in the snow. "Well, your opinion ain't the same as mine. I hate all Indians, and I especially hate Crows for stealin' my land. They all ought to be shot down like rabid dogs!"

Struggling to control his temper, Yellowstone County's sheriff stood nose to nose with the elder Van Horn and said through his teeth, "Are you aware that the Crows fought on the side of the whites and against their own kind in the Indian wars of the eighteen sixties and seventies?"

Van Horn shook his head uncertainly. "Well, no . . . I, uh—"

"Well, they did. They fought Blackfeet, Dakota, and Cheyenne. In spite of the fact that the United States government had forced the Crows onto the reservation in eighteen sixty-eight, Chief War Horse led his warriors to fight alongside the U.S. cavalry for ten years! You have no cause to hate the Crows, Barth. The federal government bought your land. The Crows did not steal it."

Van Horn's heavy jowls shook. His voice sharpened as he said, "You're not livin' on property that borders the Crow reservation, mister. I am!"

London snorted. "The Crows haven't caused you any trouble, and you and I both know it. Chief War Horse has kept his three thousand people well disciplined, and as far as your property is concerned, you have no way of knowing whether the Crows are three miles away or a thousand! Now tell me I'm wrong."

The Van Horn patriarch glared silently at the sheriff, defiance in his eyes.

When no response came, London said somberly, "Those three Crows did not start the fight, and when Chief War Horse hears about it, he'll think less of whites. I'll try to smooth it over with him, and you'd better hope I can, because War Horse can give you trouble you really don't know anything about."

Van Horn looked past the sheriff and saw that Clete and Wes had managed to revive Hale and get him on his feet. Now that the show was over, the crowd was breaking up. Looking back at London, Van Horn said, "Are you through with the sermon, Reverend?"

London replied in an even tone, "I don't want any more trouble between you and the Crows."

Van Horn made no comment. He stepped around the sheriff and helped his sons as they hoisted Hale onto his horse's back.

Hale gripped his saddle horn, steadying himself, and looked at London with undimmed hostility. "My day will come, London," he growled. "I'll get even with you."

London ignored him and called to his father, "You remember what I said, Barth."

Van Horn did not look back as he nudged his horse up the street. Neither did Clete nor Wes, but Hale turned and gave London a parting stare. There was poison in it.

It was noon, and Sheriff Matt London sat alone in his office while his deputy and Dusty Canfield ate lunch at the café across the street. He thought about the morning's incident and silently cursed Hale Van Horn. London knew that War Horse would visit him about the fight, which Hale had reportedly started. He hoped the Crow chief would let the matter die since Hale had been sufficiently beaten up.

At twelve-thirty Will Baker and Dusty Canfield entered the office. The wind was picking up, driving the cold deeper into everything on the surface of Montana's frozen face. London heard Dusty swear at the cold as he slammed the door shut. Standing up and putting on his coat, London said, "What's the matter with you, Dusty? It's only twenty below out there. I thought the cold you endured in the old days would make this feel like the tropics."

Dusty regarded the sheriff caustically. "Well, them was the old days. When a fella gets to be my age, he loses some of his heat. There's ice in my blood now."

"Just how old are you, my friend?" asked London, putting on his hat. "You never have told me."

"Old enough!" Dusty hobbled to the stove to warm his bony body.

"Old enough?"

"Old enough to know better than to ask a distinguished citizen his age."

Will Baker laughed. "You'll never get him to admit how old he is, Matt."

London headed toward the door. Putting his hand on the knob, he said, "Keep a sharp lookout for the Hatch gang. If anything unusual happens out there on the street, grab your guns and bolt the door." Grinning at the old man, he added, "That reminds me, Dusty. It's time for the stove in the cellblock to be stoked. I left the job for you."

"Thanks" was Dusty's dry reply.

London closed the door behind him and headed down the street, making a right turn at the first corner and walking toward his modest log home in the residential district. His long legs carried him quickly through the bitter wind that was whisking stinging snow at him from the rooftops.

Blue jays chattered in the naked cottonwoods in his front yard as London stepped onto the porch. He wiped his boots on the gunnysack doormat and then entered the warm house. When he smelled the aroma of hot soup that filled the air, his mouth started to water.

As he was removing his hat and coat, his wife appeared in the kitchen doorway, smiling warmly, a wooden ladle in her hand. London ran his gaze over her captivating face and small, perfect body. With a sigh he said, "There she is. Mrs. Matthew London. An all-American beauty . . . I am truly the luckiest man in the world!"

The woman standing in the doorway blushed and laughed affectionately. Then she held out her arms and glided toward her husband, her long dark hair swinging below her shoulders.

The sheriff gathered Amy London into his arms and looked down into her green eyes. Then he brought his lips to hers. The kiss was long, sweet, and tender. When their lips parted, he held her close and said, "The day you became my wife I thought I could never love you more. But we've been married three years now, and I love you a million times more."

Laying a hand to his cheek, Amy said softly, "And I, you." Amy buried her fingers in her husband's thick curly mane as he kissed her passionately.

"Is that potato soup I smell?" he asked when their lips had parted.

"Sure is," she answered with a smile, and then headed back to the kitchen. "Wash your hands, and we'll eat."

During lunch, London told Amy about the fracas in front of the Big Sky Saloon, voicing his dislike for the Van Horn men and his concern about what might happen with Chief War Horse.

"It must be hard on Myrtle and Holly to live around that boisterous bunch," Amy mused. "I wonder how Clete's wife—what's her name?"

"Sandra."

"I wonder how Sandra fits in out there."

"I don't know," said London. "But I've no doubt Sandra has found out what it's like to be kept in line by big Barth."

"He *does* rule the roost, doesn't he?"

"To put it mildly," agreed the sheriff. "You know that Will has it bad for Holly. . . ."

"Yes."

"Well, Barth was in the office this morning before the

ruckus with the Crows, and while he was there he told Will in no uncertain terms to stay away from his daughter."

Amy shook her head. "Do you think he'll listen?"

"Nope."

"That means more trouble."

"I guess Will figures she's worth it."

"Speaking of trouble," said Amy, "just how do you expect War Horse to react when his three men tell him about what the Van Horns did?"

"Not well, I assure you. I expect him to pay me a visit today or tomorrow. I'm hoping the fact that I bloodied Hale up will help the situation."

Amy smiled thinly. "Let's hope the friendship and trust that you and War Horse have developed will prevent this from becoming a major incident."

London thought back over the six years he had been sheriff of Yellowstone County. On occasions when Crow braves had gotten drunk and caused trouble in Billings, he had turned them over to War Horse for punishment and discipline. By the same token, when white men had committed crimes against the Crows, War Horse had always let the sheriff handle them. London had never failed to follow through, seeing to it that justice was done. Not only did the two men trust each other, but War Horse had also taught his people to trust Matt London.

There had been few problems with the Crow under War Horse's leadership, and the tribe had stayed within the law. The United States government had allowed the Crow to keep their weapons, but only for hunting. They had agreed in the treaty never to use them in an offensive way against white men. Matt London, however, always felt a bit of uneasiness in the back of his mind. There was a limit to what War Horse would take from whites, and such troublemakers as the Van Horns had the potential for provoking the chief to use violence.

Amy poured her husband a fresh cup of coffee. Changing the subject, she said, "Matt, what about Ruben Hatch? Do you think you'll have trouble from his gang?"

"I expect it," he replied morosely. "I'm not allowing him to be left alone in the jail until he hangs. Dusty's going to sleep there every night. If the gang hasn't shown up by the day of the hanging, I'll have a number of armed townsmen standing by so that Hatch will be surrounded when he walks to the gallows."

Amy's face was etched with worry. Visibly nervous, she reached across the table and took hold of his hand. "You will be careful, won't you? Remember what happened with Buford Way."

London thought back some two years. He had captured outlaw Buford Way and taken him to trial, and the jury had convicted him of murder. The judge had sentenced him to hang, but Way's gang had stormed into Billings with blazing guns, attempting to save their leader from the noose. During the gunfight, the sheriff had taken a bullet in the left shoulder.

London patted Amy's hand. "I'll be careful, honey, but you've got to realize that this sort of thing goes along with my job. In spite of what his gang did, Buford Way went to the gallows on schedule, and Ruben Hatch will also hang on schedule. Besides, we've got Dusty with us this time. He's a tough old bird, and since he was a lawman once, he's got plenty of experience. And like I said, if the gang doesn't show up by hanging day, I'll have plenty of men around ready for anything that might happen."

Amy stood up, circled the table, and laid her hands on London's shoulders. With a shaky voice she said, "I just don't want them to dig any more bullets out of you—or worse yet, see you buried."

London took hold of one of her hands, scooted his chair back, and stood. "No gang of outlaws is going to separate us. We've got a lifetime before us, I promise."

He kissed her, and the thrill of it seemed to take Amy's breath away. When the kiss ended, she sharply drew in air, and as her husband cupped her face in his hands, tears began to spill down her cheeks. "Oh, Matt. I wouldn't want to live if anything happened to you. Without you it wouldn't be a life; it would only be a drab existence."

Wiping her tears away with his thumbs, London looked deep into her eyes. "Nothing's going to happen, honey. You're stuck with me the rest of your life."

She managed a smile and then said, "I like being stuck with you."

He held her tight for several minutes and then kissed her briefly. "I've got to get back to the office now."

Amy stood on the porch in the cold air and watched her husband until he passed from sight. Sighing deeply, she rubbed her arms, then turned and entered the log house, closing the door quietly.

Chapter Three

That afternoon Barth Van Horn and his three oldest sons huddled behind a snow-covered mound some ten miles northeast of Billings near the road to Miles City. The merciless wind knifed them with raw fury. Squinting against the icy particles of snow that pricked their cold faces, they studied the outline of the wagon-rutted road. Soon the stagecoach from Miles City would appear.

Speaking to his father, Wes Van Horn said, "You think Ma and the girls will ever forgive us for this?"

Barth Van Horn beat his gloved hands together and replied, "They're plenty hot about it right now, but they'll get over it when we bring home the twenty thousand."

"Maybe we shouldn't have told them about it till after we robbed the stage, Pa," suggested Clete.

"Don't make no difference, son. They'd holler just as loud either time. Don't you boys worry about the women. They'll get over it. We're doin' the right thing by fixin' ourselves up financially. It was the stinkin' government that made us give up our land to the Crows for a song, wasn't it? Well, the twenty thousand on that stagecoach is government money! Things balance out in time, even though London took the reward money." Van Horn cursed.

Hale, standing aloof from the others, stomped his feet and worked his arms to ward off the cold. Hunching deeper into his heavy sheepskin coat, he swore vehemently.

Anger twisted the elder Van Horn's face as he snarled,

"You act like you got a burr in the seat of your britches. What's eatin' you, boy?"

"You could've picked a warmer day to rob a stage-coach," snapped Hale.

"I don't like this cold any better than you do," Barth Van Horn retorted. "Neither do your brothers, but you don't hear them gripin'. The money ridin' that stage ain't gonna be there on another day. It's today or never. Now the best thing for you to do is shut up."

Hale bristled. He was no longer a child, and he did not like being treated like one. "Well, it ain't worth twenty thousand to freeze. Ain't *no* money worth gettin' frostbit over."

Barth Van Horn stepped close to his oldest son. His eyes were flinty as he glared at Hale and roared, "When I tell you to shut up, you shut up, y'hear?"

Hale felt defiance, hard and explosive, well up within him. He met his father's glare with his own pale blue eyes as the silence stretched between them. Even though Hale matched his father's six feet four inches and two hundred thirty pounds, he was not sure he could handle him. Barth Van Horn, hard and tough in spite of the paunch that the years had put on him, was unmercifully brutal when he was angry. He ruled with an iron hand, dominating his large family. Though he was tender toward his ailing wife and watched over his daughter, Holly, like a mother hen, he angered like a teased bull when his authority was challenged.

Hale quickly decided to knuckle under, as he always had. Though it went hard against his grain, he dropped his eyes and said, "I ain't gonna argue, Pa. I spoke my piece. Let's drop it."

Grinning triumphantly, Van Horn said, "That's more like it. Now let's concentrate on takin' that stage."

While they waited, Van Horn reminded his sons that the horses had to be kept completely out of sight. Though the Van Horns would be wearing masks, the robbery victims could possibly identify them later if they got a good look at their mounts.

To that the senior Van Horn added, "I don't want no shootin' unless somebody on that stage tries to throw a gun on us. We ain't murderers." When the three sons had agreed, he continued, "And remember, we want 'em to think we're from Ruben Hatch's gang. So you boys follow my lead, okay?"

Hale smirked. "Good thinkin'. We get the money and the Hatch gang gets the blame."

Clete and Wes laughed, agreeing to go along with the ruse.

Time dragged on. The sun darted in and out from behind swirling clouds, alternating dull light and sharp glare when the sun's rays hit the snow. The merciless wind lashed at them. At times they had to shield their eyes from the icy crystals that were assaulting them from the snow-covered mound in front of them. Silently they cursed the numbing cold and then thought of the huge potbellied stove in their big farmhouse.

Suddenly they spotted movement on the white mantled plains to the northeast. Within seconds it materialized into a stagecoach with six horses pulling it through the snow. As the stage drew within a mile and dropped into a shallow ravine, Van Horn said, "All right, boys. Get in position."

Hale pulled up his scarf to cover his nose and mouth and headed over the mound to the parallel wheel tracks that identified the road. He drew his revolver and lay facedown in the snow between the tracks while the other Van Horns hunkered low behind the mound, masking their faces. Hale took a quick look to make sure the horses could not be seen from the road.

Shortly the metallic sound of harness, along with the blowing of laboring horses, rode the wind. Hale tensed as he heard one of the men up in the box say to the other one, "Hey, Ollie! Look down there! Some poor fella is layin' in the middle of the road!"

"Whoa!" cried the one named Ollie, pulling back on the reins.

A male voice from inside the coach called out, "What is it?"

"Man layin' in the middle of the road," answered the driver.

"I'll check on him," volunteered the shotgunner, leaving his seat on the box and slipping to the ground.

"Be careful, Bill," called the driver. "Could be a trick."

Trudging through the snow, the shotgunner called over his shoulder, "Don't think so. Doesn't look like he's breathin'."

The shotgunner carried his double-barreled weapon with him. Reaching the inert man, he knelt down and with his free hand turned Hale over. Instantly Hale snapped back the hammer of his revolver and aimed it at Bill's face.

The shotgunner gasped, dropping his gun in the snow and throwing up his hands.

The driver started to pull the gun from his hip but checked himself when three bulky masked men came up from the gully, guns drawn.

"Throw the gun down!" barked one of the men.

The driver obeyed, thrusting his hands in the air.

Hale peered over his mask at the shotgunner and, keeping the gun aimed at his face, said, "Climb up fast and open the strongbox, mister."

"We don't have any money in the strongbox. We—"

Hale's free hand balled into a fist and struck the shotgunner on the nose. The man went down hard, blood spurting from his nostrils. Looming over him, Hale rasped, "I know what's in your strongbox. Now let's go up and open it."

The shotgunner, running a hand under his bleeding nose, groped his way to a standing position. He quickly stumbled to the coach, stepped up on the wheel, and lifted up the driver's seat to expose the large strongbox bolted to the floor. When the shotgunner said, "I ain't got the key to the padlock," Barth Van Horn climbed up beside him and, thumbing back the hammer of his revolver, shot off the lock that held the lid secure. Van Horn eagerly bent over and began to lift open the box.

Hale waved his gun at the shotgunner and barked, "Get down here beside the driver, mister. And keep your hands in the air."

Three elderly men and a middle-aged woman, their faces pale with fear, were still aboard the stage. Clete kept his eyes on them while Wes kept his gun trained on the driver and shotgunner.

Barth Van Horn slammed down the lid of the strongbox and swore vehemently. "This thing doesn't have any twenty thousand dollars in it!" he said angrily.

"I told you there's no cash in it, mister," spoke up the shotgunner.

Van Horn's angry eyes widened over the top of his mask. He bellowed at the driver, "You've got another one hidden. Now save yourself a lot of trouble and tell us where it is!"

"There's no other one, mister," responded the driver. "The Army was notified that the Fargo agent in Billings was murdered. As a precaution they took the money off the stage at Miles City. You can search the coach, but I'm telling you the truth."

Hale, standing near his father, swore and said, "What now?"

Van Horn hesitated, blinded with anger. He had counted on having the twenty thousand in his hands by now. Finding his voice, he said, "Let's get what we can from the passengers." Remembering his plan to throw blame for the robbery on the Hatch gang, he added, "Then we gotta figure a way to get Ruben out of jail."

"Yeah!" said Hale, picking up on the cue. "But Hatch ain't gonna be happy that we missed the twenty thousand."

"Maybe we'd better leave him in jail," put in Wes, aiding the ruse. "Then we won't have to worry about him."

"Hah!" joined in Clete. "If you believe that, you don't know Ruben Hatch. He'd get out sooner or later and kill every one of us."

"Well, let's see what the passengers have to offer," said Hale, jerking the coach door open. "Everybody out!"

The three elderly men and the middle-aged woman removed the thick buffalo-hide blankets that covered them and filed out into the cold. The woman was shaking with fear.

While Barth and Wes held their guns on the driver and shotgunner, Hale said to Clete, "Clean out the woman's purse."

The frightened woman squealed with fright and indignation as Clete Van Horn snatched the purse from her hand. While he was going through it, Hale said, "All right, gents, give me your wallets."

Two of them quickly did so, but the third old man said shakily, "I don't have mine with me."

As Hale stuffed the wallets in his coat pocket, he said gruffly, "Don't lie to me, mister. The shotgunner got a bloody nose for doin' that. You'll get worse. Now hand over your wallet."

"I told you, I don't have it with me," replied the old man. "Go ahead, search me. See for yourself."

"Hurry it up!" Barth Van Horn shouted at Hale. "We've got to get out of here."

Hale did not look at his father. Moving his nose close to the old man's leathery face, he said, "I'm gonna look inside the coach, Grandpa. If I find your wallet in there, you are a dead man!"

The old gent's features blanched. Hale saw it and with a wicked grin dived into the coach. After he had tossed the buffalo blankets out the door, he ran his fingers along the sides of the seats. Blurting a profanity, he backed out of the stage and shook a fat wallet in the face of the old man. Eyes wild, he raged, "Don't have it with you, huh? You lied to me, Grandpa!"

Hale sank his gloved fingers into the old man's coat and flung him to the ground. Dropping to his knees, Hale straddled him. The hammer of his revolver was already cocked as he jammed the muzzle against the man's forehead and snarled, "You better pray, Grandpa. You've got five seconds to live."

Hale Van Horn's words carried a flat finality. The old man's face was a mask of stark terror, and he shook his head back and forth as if to convince Hale not to go through with the killing.

"No!" Barth Van Horn shouted. "Let him go!"

Hale turned and looked at his father, whose voice was thick as he repeated, "Let him go!"

Barth Van Horn watched as Hale dragged his free hand across his eyes and blinked as if considering the consequences of disobeying his father's command.

"I said let him go! *Now!*" his father's voice thundered.

Hale tightened his jaw, pressing the muzzle of his revolver hard against the old man's forehead. "He lied to me!"

"You have his wallet, don't you? Forget him. He's just a helpless old man. He's done you no harm."

Hale's face showed red above his neck. Malevolence was in his ice-blue eyes. Ignoring his father, he glared down at the terrorized old man and growled, "You shouldn't have lied to me!" He dropped the hammer, and the gun roared and bucked in his hand. The bullet centered the old man's forehead, ripping through his skull and spraying blood on the snow.

The woman screamed and fainted, collapsing in a heap. While the howling wind carried the gun smoke away, Hale stood up. His brothers, wide-eyed with disbelief, looked at him, and Barth Van Horn's angry stare seemed to bore right through his oldest son. He was ready to beat Hale until he could not walk, but then what conscience he had left reminded him that none of this would have happened if he had not led his sons to this place. Turning about, he barked at the shotgunner and driver to load the dead man and the unconscious woman into the coach and head back for Miles City. He warned that he and the rest of the Hatch gang would be staying close to Billings. If any of the passengers showed up there, they would be shot on sight.

When the stagecoach had disappeared on the northeastern horizon, Barth said above the howl of the wind, "Let's get our horses and go home."

When they had mounted, the old man set his hard glare on Hale and said crisply, "Don't you ever go against me again!"

When his father and brothers had turned their mounts in the direction of the farm, Hale stared at their backs and spit disgustedly in the snow. Mumbling to himself, he waited for a long moment, then spurred his horse hard to catch up with them.

Earlier that day, while the four Van Horns were entering Billings to see Sheriff Matt London about their reward, two young Crow Indians were riding on the reservation a mile southeast of Billings.

Carrying rifles and cloaked in heavy furs, they bent their heads against the driving wind and let their dark eyes search the snow-covered land for antelope. The one who wore a length of rope looped over his shoulder was Leaning Tree, twenty-year-old son of War Horse, chief of the Crow nation. The other was Yellow Bird, Leaning Tree's best friend, who was a year younger.

Squinting against the glare and the cold wind, the young men rode slowly over the rolling land, alert for the sight of antelope. Both Indians tensed as a jackrabbit appeared from out of nowhere and scampered across the ground, leaving tracks in the thin white crust. Within seconds it was out of sight.

Leaning Tree looked at his friend and smiled as he said in his native tongue, "Maybe we should have shot the rabbit. The antelope seem to be hiding today."

Returning the smile, Yellow Bird nodded, and then he gazed at the hilly plains around them. He felt certain they would spot antelope soon. They just needed to be patient.

As they slowly continued to make their way through the snow on their pintos, they came upon a small creek. It was frozen over, but they could hear the water gurgling underneath the ice. Along its banks cottonwood trees stretched barren branches toward the sun as if to beg for warmth. Abruptly a large male pheasant darted from its cover and hurried across the snow, wings flapping, startling the intruders.

Leaning Tree and Yellow Bird veered their pintos down the creek bank, and as the animals crossed the frozen surface of the creek, their unshod hooves cracked through the thin ice. The two Indians allowed their mounts to lap up the cold water for a few minutes before climbing the snow-covered bank on the opposite side. Then the Indians headed toward the small forest that marked the reservation's northern border.

After riding some two hundred yards, the young men spotted an antelope buck chewing on the bark of a tree at the edge of the woods. The animal was facing away from the riders, and he was unaware of their downwind approach. Pulling their horses to a halt, the Indians quietly slid to the ground. Leaning Tree nodded to his friend, who understood his intention. Yellow Bird shouldered his rifle and sighted in on the antelope, which stood about a hundred and fifty yards away.

While Yellow Bird drew his bead, Leaning Tree watched the magnificent buck. It was a typical pronghorn with a reddish-brown coat, a short dark-brown mane, a white belly, and a rounded light-colored spot on its rump, which produced a flash of white when danger approached, serving as a warning signal to other antelopes. On its stately head were a pair of erect horns, each branching into two prongs, the longer curving backward, the shorter projecting forward.

A split second before Yellow Bird squeezed the trigger, the buck pivoted, flashing the white hairs on its rump. As the crack of the rifle echoed across the snow-laden prairie, the antelope went down with a bullet in the left shoulder. Yellow Bird had been aiming for the rib cage, hoping to send the bullet into the heart, and he knew he had missed the mark when the buck scrambled up and began running into the trees, limping severely.

"Hurry, Yellow Bird!" shouted Leaning Tree, leaping onto his pinto's back. "We must catch him!"

The two Indians galloped for the trees, pushing their horses until they were almost clear of the forest. The antelope angled across the rolling land in a northeasterly direction, falling twice as it stumbled on. Leaning Tree and Yellow Bird watched helplessly as the wounded animal approached a dry gulch that served as the borderline between the reservation and private property. When the antelope had crossed it, the Indians drew rein and looked at each other with despair: It was against federal law for them to hunt off the reservation.

The breath from the nostrils of their panting horses formed small clouds, then dissipated in the cold air. Yellow Bird said to his friend, "That is the Van Horn farm. What should we do now?"

Leaning Tree bit down on his lower lip. He knew that the Van Horns had hostile feelings toward his people, stemming from the recent government takeover of some Van Horn land for addition to the Crow reservation, which adjoined their property. To follow the antelope onto Van Horn property could lead to trouble, Leaning Tree thought. Shaking his head, he replied, "This is a bad situation, Yellow Bird. It is our ancient law that we must never allow a wounded animal to suffer a slow, painful death. I must show mercy to the antelope. I will pursue it and do it the honor of taking its life."

Yellow Bird's dark face clouded with fear. "But what about the white man's law that forbids our hunting on his lands, Leaning Tree? Is it not against the law of our people to break our word? We have a treaty with the white man. We must not go against it by hunting on his land. Especially the land of Barth Van Horn. He is full of hatred. He might bring in soldiers."

Indecision showed in Leaning Tree's eyes. The wind plucked at the heavy fur hood on his head as he sat and watched the antelope fall again. The wounded animal lay there for a moment and then rose to its feet, faltering onward. Speaking in a monotone, Leaning Tree said, "My mind is made up, but you must come to your own conclusion, Yellow Bird. Is it better to break the ancient law of the Crow and thereby disobey my father, or to break the white man's law? The antelope will suffer for many hours—perhaps days—before it dies."

After a brief pause Yellow Bird responded, "The animal must not be allowed to suffer, my friend. Obedience to War Horse and our ancient law is most important."

Leaning Tree smiled warmly at his friend, and then prodding their mounts onto the Van Horn farm, the two young men took off in pursuit of the antelope.

Four miles northeast of Billings at the Van Horn farm, Holly Van Horn was helping her ailing mother, Myrtle, into a chair at the big kitchen table. Sandra Van Horn, Clete's twenty-five-year-old wife, finished setting bowls of hot stew on the table and sat down next to her mother-in-law. Across the table were twenty-two-year-old Sam and twenty-year-old Ben, both of whom were as large as their father and older brothers. Absent at the moment was thin and wiry Jimmy Van Horn, at sixteen the youngest of the family.

As they began eating, Myrtle eyed Jimmy's empty place and said, "Where's the boy?"

"He'll be here in a moment," volunteered Ben. "He's still getting washed up." Everyone knew if their father were present, Jimmy would be in deep trouble for being late to the table.

Blond Holly's lovely features were solemn. Looking at her mother, she asked, "What are you going to say to Pa when he and the boys return?"

"Nothing," replied Myrtle sharply. "I've already told your father what I think of this robbing business. When they come home, I don't want anybody at this table to ask them if they have the money. I don't want the subject brought up at all. You boys tell Jimmy I said so. We do not discuss the shameful blight that has come to this family!"

At that moment tousle-headed Jimmy appeared and moved quickly to the table. Casting a furtive look at his brothers, he placed his skinny rump on the hard seat of his chair and said, "I don't know why Pa wants us to build the chicken coop now. Why can't we wait till spring?"

Myrtle, her pinched face aged by far more than her fifty-nine years, looked at her son. With resignation in her voice she said, "Jimmy, there's no use questioning your father's orders. Just do what he tells you."

"And don't be slow in eatin', Jim," said Sam. "When Ben and I are done, you're done. We're all going out that door together to work."

"Seems like it's takin' forever to get that darn coop built," complained Jimmy.

"Pa and the boys will be back soon, son," their frail mother said. "They'll be pitching in to help."

"Won't really matter," said the young man, running a hand through his blond hair. "Pa will just come up with some other project to keep us working out in the cold."

For several minutes there was only the sound of clinking forks, but then Holly turned to her pretty sister-in-law. "Sandra, how's your new dress coming along? The fabric is so pretty."

Sandra tossed her long dark hair and replied, "I think I'll have it done this afternoon."

Ben snickered. "You wantin' to wear it to impress someone, Holly?"

Holly narrowed her blue eyes. "Sandra is a good two inches shorter than I am, Ben. Her dress wouldn't fit me right."

"What are you doing this afternoon, Holly?" asked Sandra.

The blond-haired woman smiled and said, "I'm going to strap on my Colts and do a little target practice."

Jimmy looked astonished. "You're gonna go out in the cold when you don't have to?"

Holly giggled. "It's not that bad."

"County fair isn't until May, Holly," put in Sam. "Why are you practicin' now?"

"I don't want to get rusty," she replied flatly. "If I'm going to improve, I must stay at it all the time."

Jimmy said, "Next election, you ought to run for sheriff. I'll bet you can outshoot Matt London."

"She'd like that," Sandra said, laughing. "Then she could work real close to Will Baker."

Holly blushed, but at the sound of the deputy's name her eyes had taken on a dreamy cast.

"Seen him lately?" Sandra asked her sister-in-law.

"Not for three days."

"Why didn't you go to the barn dance with Jerry Pemberton, Holly?" asked Ben. "I know he asked you."

Holly stiffened and said curtly, "If I couldn't go to the dance with Will Baker, I didn't want to go with anyone."

Ben eased back in his chair. "You might as well forget the deputy, little sister. As long as Baker wears that badge, Pa won't let him court you."

Holly looked away from her brother. She knew what Ben was saying was true. Her father hated lawmen. Ever since she was a little girl, he had emphatically urged his children never to trust a lawman, and his tirades had grown even more rancorous following the death of his brother—a death that he blamed on a lawman. They were out for themselves first more often than not, he said, and would be quicker to take a bribe and look the other way than to draw a gun.

Privately Holly's mother had explained to her that Barth Van Horn's brother, a bounty hunter, had been killed because of a sheriff's double-dealing. After the brother, Herb, had brought in a desperate criminal, the prisoner's gang had offered the sheriff a substantial sum of money to release his prisoner—or to be elsewhere when the gang staged an escape for their leader. Once the gang leader was out, he and his men had tracked Herb Van Horn and brutally murdered him, leaving a note pinned to the dead man's shirt that implicated the sheriff in the outlaw's escape.

But Barth Van Horn's contempt for lawmen could not change how Holly felt toward Will Baker. He had captured her heart, and she did not want it to be any different.

Rising from the table, Sam said to his brothers, "Well, let's get to work." The three men climbed into their heavy coats, pulled on their hats, and headed over to the half-built chicken coop. As they went to work, the raw cold of Montana's plains seemed not to bother the two older brothers, but Jimmy felt it penetrate right through to his joints.

They had been working for almost twenty minutes when Jimmy looked toward the west pasture, where some movement had caught his eye. It was a young antelope buck, limping across the field about three hundred yards out. He saw the buck fall in the snow, then rise again. "Hey, fellas!" he said to his brothers, pointing toward the animal. "Look."

Following Jimmy's finger, Sam and Ben looked out at the stumbling antelope. "Must be sick or hurt," commented Ben.

But at that instant two rifle shots clattered across the prairie, and the buck fell dead. The Van Horn brothers saw two Crow Indians ride out of the brush, rifles smoking. Sam swore. "I can't believe what I'm seein'. Those dirty Crows are huntin' game on our property!"

"Not for long, they ain't!" exclaimed Ben. "Let's get our guns."

Before following his brothers, Jimmy Van Horn hesitated briefly and watched as the two Indians dismounted and knelt down to examine the antelope. Then the youngest Van Horn headed back toward the house.

The women were not in sight when the three brothers dashed to their rooms. Seconds later they were bolting back through the door, levering cartridges into the chambers of their rifles.

Leaning Tree and Yellow Bird knelt beside the dead antelope, relieved to know that it would suffer no more.

After making certain that it was indeed dead, Leaning Tree rose and said to his friend in their native tongue, "We must give the buck to the Van Horn family since we have shot it on their property. They will understand when we explain what happened."

Yellow Bird agreed. Taking the length of rope that was looped over his shoulder, Leaning Tree tied it around the hind legs of the dead animal, intending to drag it across the field to the Van Horn house.

Leaning Tree was just cinching the knot when Yellow Bird touched his friend's shoulder and said, "The Van Horns . . ."

Looking up, Leaning Tree saw Sam, Ben, and Jimmy coming toward them, holding their rifles in ready position. They were within twenty yards and moving fast with Sam in the lead. "Stay calm," Leaning Tree whispered.

Yellow Bird swallowed hard.

"Hold it right there!" Sam yelled, sighting his gun barrel on Leaning Tree's chest. "What are you Crows doin' huntin' on our property?"

In a low, level voice Leaning Tree said in the white man's tongue, "I am Leaning Tree, son of War Horse. This is Yellow Bird. We—"

"I didn't ask who you were!" bellowed Sam, a mottled flush stamping his heavy cheeks. "I asked why you stinkin' Indians are huntin' on Van Horn property!"

The hostility in Sam's words told the Indians that he was not going to be easily convinced by their story. Keeping his tone low, Leaning Tree replied, "Yellow Bird shot antelope on reservation but not kill it. We followed injured animal onto Van Horn land to finish the kill."

Sam snarled, "You've broken United States government law. Do you realize that?"

"We not mean to break law," said Yellow Bird. "But—"

"But nothin'!" Sam half screamed. "You know the law! You agreed to a treaty! You just broke it. That's bad enough. But now to come on *our* property . . . Just who do you think you are, trespassin' on Van Horn land as if you owned it?"

Leaning Tree wanted to tell the insolent man that before the white men had come in great numbers and stolen the land from the Indians, it belonged to the Crows. But knowing that would only add fuel to Sam's fire, he said instead, "My father, War Horse, taught ancient Crow law: Never allow wounded animal to die slow, painful death. Animal must be followed, killed, at any cost. Yellow Bird and I tracked antelope onto your land only to give it merciful death. We were about to bring antelope to Van Horns, since antelope died on Van Horn property."

Anger danced dangerously in Sam Van Horn's pale blue eyes. Pointing a stiff finger, he rasped, "You're a liar, Leaning Tree. The two of you will pay for this."

Working his arms against the cold, Jimmy said, "What are we gonna do with them?"

"I'd like to shoot 'em on the spot," responded Sam, "but we'd best wait till Pa gets home."

"Our story true," Leaning Tree said curtly, anger slowly creeping through him. "You will find three bullets in antelope. You not hear two shots when we killed it?"

"I didn't count 'em."

"Follow antelope's trail," Leaning Tree said, swinging a hand in the direction from which the buck had come.

"Don't prove nothin'," Sam said caustically. "Get their guns, Jimmy."

While the youth picked up their rifles from the snow, Sam barked, "Okay, head for the house."

Leaning Tree and Yellow Bird were ushered at gunpoint to a spot near the back of the house. Some forty feet from the back porch they were forced to sit on the cold, snow-covered ground beneath the naked limbs of a huge cottonwood tree. Ben tied their pintos nearby.

Holly Van Horn came out of the house wearing a short-waisted sheepskin coat and two Colt .45's strapped to her slender hips. She stopped short at the edge of the porch, surprised at the sight that met her eyes. The wind plucked at her blond tresses as she looked at her brothers and demanded sharply, "What's going on here?"

The door opened behind Holly, and Sandra stepped out, slipping into a heavy coat and flanking her sister-in-law.

Bobbing his head toward the Indians, Sam said, "We caught these stinkin' redskins trespassin' on our land."

Ben added, "Yeah. These two savages crossed right over the reservation line and shot that antelope on our property."

Holly saw the dead buck lying behind the pinto ponies. Her attention was drawn away from it when Leaning Tree said, "You also a Van Horn, ma'am?"

Holly nodded.

Leaning Tree introduced himself as War Horse's son and told her Yellow Bird's name. He explained the situation briefly, telling her the truth of the matter. While Leaning Tree was speaking, Myrtle Van Horn appeared on the porch bundled in a heavy shawl. She, too, listened intently to the Indian's story.

When Leaning Tree had finished, Myrtle said above the whine of the wind, "His explanation sounds reasonable to me, Sam. Let them go home."

Holly and Sandra looked at Myrtle, then at Sam, nodding in agreement.

Ben spoke up. "You women go on back in the house. This is men's business."

In the same cutting tone Sam said, "We're holdin' these Crows till Pa gets home. He'll be the one to decide what happens to these trespassers."

"They're not trespassers and you know it!" said Holly. "Do what Ma tells you. Nothing but trouble can come if you involve Pa." Stepping off the porch, she walked over to Sam. "Let them go right now and pretend the incident never happened. Let them take the buck too. By rights, it's theirs."

Sam bristled, looking down his nose at his sister. "You may be fool enough to believe these red-skinned liars, but me and Ben and Jimmy ain't. They trespassed on our land, and they're gonna be dealt with."

Holly shuddered, a premonition of disaster growing in her mind. She knew tragedy would be inevitable if her father got involved. Stepping past her brothers, she walked to where the Indians sat in the snow and said, "Leaning

Tree, Yellow Bird, take your antelope and leave. Right now."

Sam made a threatening sound that reminded Holly of a growl. Stepping up from behind, he grabbed her and spun her around, then slapped her hard. The force of the blow knocked her to the ground.

Both Indians tensed and began to rise. "Hold it right there!" bellowed Ben, waving the muzzle of the rifle between them. "Move another muscle and I'll send you to your happy hunting ground."

Myrtle Van Horn's knees buckled. Sandra had to grip her with both hands.

Jimmy shouted at Sam, "Pa will break your skull for manhandlin' Holly!"

Sam retorted, "When Pa knows the situation, he'll agree that I did the right thing!"

Holly stood, rubbing her face where a welt was forming. Glaring at her brother, she said heatedly, "I could pull these guns and shoot your ears off! You know that, don't you?"

Sam laughed defiantly. "Yeah. You could. But you won't. I'm your brother. You wouldn't shoot your brother."

Chapter Four

As Barth Van Horn and his three oldest sons rode toward home, they talked of how they had come up empty in their attempted robbery of the payroll. What they had taken from the passengers did not amount to much, they found after going through the wallets. No one mentioned Hale's cold-blooded murder of the old man.

Hunkering deep into their coats to stay warm, they rode silently for several moments, then Barth Van Horn spoke up and said, "Boys, what would you say to robbin' a bank? Since we didn't get the twenty thousand or the reward money and couldn't borrow any, it looks like we gotta steal it."

"My vote is with you, Pa," said Hale. "You got a particular bank in mind?"

"Yeah." The big man grinned. "Merchants Bank down in Sheridan. There's money in that town."

When Hale showed enthusiasm at the prospect of robbing the bank in Sheridan, Wyoming, Barth Van Horn said he would give it some thought and talk to him about it later. The conversation trailed off as they rode onto their ranch and headed for the house. When Barth Van Horn looked toward the framework of the new chicken coop and saw that no one was working on it, he grew livid. "Those three lazy whelps are layin' down on the job. Not one of them is workin'."

The moment they rounded the house, they saw the

dead antelope, the two pintos, the Indians sitting on the snow-covered ground, and his three youngest sons standing over the two Indians, holding guns on them. The women were nowhere in sight.

Drawing up to his younger sons, Barth Van Horn eyed them with puzzlement and said in his blustering voice, "What's this?"

As the four riders dismounted, Sam answered, "These Crows were huntin' on our property, Pa."

Van Horn regarded the Indians with a cold, black stare and then turned back to Sam. "They killed the antelope on our land?"

A triumphant look was in Sam's eyes. "Caught 'em red-handed, trespassin'."

Barth Van Horn's hatred for the Crows who had taken his property was unleashed. Raging, he stomped to the Indians and stood towering over them, a stiff and enormous figure in the midafternoon sun. "Don't you know where the borderline of the reservation is?" he roared.

With trepidation in his dark eyes Leaning Tree looked up at the blocky shape and said, "Your son not tell you whole truth, Mr. Van Horn. Leaning Tree explain—"

His words were cut short as Sam charged over and kicked Leaning Tree savagely in the mouth, flattening him on the ground. The young Indian lay there, shaking his head, trying to clear it. His lips were split and bleeding. Yellow Bird knelt beside him, attempting to help.

Holly, Sandra, and Myrtle were filing onto the porch from inside as Van Horn clapped a hand on Sam's shoulder and said, "Good work, son. I'm proud of you three for capturin' this scum."

Holly saw Leaning Tree, his mouth bleeding, sit up with Yellow Bird's help, and immediately she knew what was happening. Running to her father, she said, "You mustn't do anything to these Indians, Pa. Have you let them tell their side of the story?"

"Sam told me what happened."

"Then I'll tell you their side of it," she said reasonably.

"What they said makes sense." She went on to recount the story exactly as Leaning Tree had told it.

"That's only the lyin' Crows' story," Sam said when she had finished. "You'd think Holly'd stand up for us, but she's takin' the side of those filthy Indians."

Van Horn looked at Holly, finally noticing the purpling bruise on her cheek. He gently cupped her chin in his hands, tilting her face. "What happened, honey? How'd you get that bruise?"

Holly's fingers went to the bruise. "Oh, it's nothing," she said nervously.

"I want to know how that happened," he demanded. "Did one of these Indians touch you?"

From the porch, Sandra spoke up loudly. "Sam hit her, Pa! That's what happened."

Van Horn's big head whirled around toward Sam. Blood flushed the sides of his neck. "You struck your sister?"

Sam threw Sandra a venomous look before facing his father. "I had to," he said defensively. "She wanted to let the redskins go. I told her that you should be the one to decide what to do with them, but she just up and walked over to them Indians and told them to leave. I . . . I had to slap her to stop what she was doin'."

Barth Van Horn had a quick temper, and at that moment it burst forth like water from a ruptured dam. His face reddening with anger, he stormed, "Boy, I taught you all your life not to hit a female. Especially your sister. Now, she was wrong in tellin' the Crows they could leave, but that gave you no cause to hit her!"

Sam's temper also erupted, and he gritted his teeth as he blurted, "I had a right to hit her because what she was doin' was wrong! I'm sick and tired of—"

Barth Van Horn's fist lashed out and struck his son. Sam's feet left the ground, and he landed flat on his back.

The two young Indians looked at each other in amazement, shocked that a father and son would fight each other. Such a thing was unheard of among their people.

The senior Van Horn stood over Sam while the other

family members looked on in silence. His lips twisted in fury, the older man said, "Don't ever talk back to me, boy!"

Sam shook his head and rolled to his knees.

Van Horn scowled and added, "As long as there's breath in my body, I'm boss around here! You understand that? You *ever* hit a woman again, I'll knock your head clean off!"

Sam Van Horn staggered to his feet, wiping blood from his mouth. He knew he could not get the best of his powerful father, and the urge to retaliate soon drained away.

His face still rigid with anger, Van Horn growled, "You apologize to your sister for hittin' her. Right now!"

Still wiping blood, Sam turned his hulking frame toward his sister and said, "I'm sorry, Holly."

She nodded her acceptance.

Van Horn then turned to the Crows. "You stinkin' savages have got to be punished for what you did."

From her place on the porch Myrtle Van Horn said in her weak voice, "Barth, I believe the Indians are telling the truth. Let them go on back to their village."

"Ma's right," put in Sandra. "You should let them go."

Clete threw his wife a scathing look that communicated his feeling that she should not be speaking up at a time such as this.

Despite what the women said, Barth Van Horn's hatred for Indians compelled him to teach them a lesson for riding onto his land. They should have let the antelope go, he thought. Speaking kindly to his ailing wife, he said, "Ma, I'll handle the situation the way I think best. Take Holly and Sandra and go into the house. This is too much excitement for your heart."

Reluctantly the three women headed into the house, but when Holly reached the door, she looked back at her father. Van Horn caught the look in her eyes. She was wordlessly telling him that trouble would come from whatever he was about to do.

Van Horn turned to his six sons. "Let's go over to the barn. I want to talk privately." Turning to the Indians, he called, "You two move a muscle and you're dead. I'm takin' my rifle, and I'll have it ready to use if I need to."

The seven men gathered beside the barn where they could keep an eye on Leaning Tree and Yellow Bird. Speaking in a low tone, Van Horn said, "I'd like to kill those red-skinned varmints, but their crime isn't bad enough to warrant that. Tell you what I *am* gonna do—I'm gonna throw a good scare into them before I let them go."

He explained his plan. While the Indians watched, the Van Horns would make hangman's nooses at the ends of two long ropes. They would tie the Indians' hands behind their backs, hoist them up onto their pintos, then place them directly under the big cottonwood. Barth Van Horn would personally cinch the nooses around their necks and then sling the ropes over the large thick limb that was about ten feet up.

With the Indians facing away from the tree Van Horn would call out for a couple of the boys to anchor the ends of the ropes to a smaller tree next to the cottonwood. But in actuality his sons would just drape the ropes over the lower limbs of it without tying them.

Van Horn further explained that he would make a fiery speech about dirty Indians who have the gall to sneak onto a white man's land and shoot his game. When he felt that the Crows were sufficiently frightened, he would slap the rumps of the pintos. The two Indians would have a moment of terror, but the ropes would simply slide over the limbs of the small tree and sail over the huge limb of the cottonwood. No harm would be done to the Indians, but they would learn not to trespass on Van Horn property.

Hale snickered. "Hey, that's pretty good, Pa. I'd sure like to be able to read their minds when their horses lurch!"

The Van Horn men had a good laugh together, and then Barth Van Horn sent Hale into the barn to get the ropes. The sun was lowering in the western sky as the father and sons stood before Leaning Tree and Yellow Bird, forming hangman's nooses.

There was fear on the faces of the young Crows as Leaning Tree said, "Barth Van Horn must not do this. Yellow Bird and I not deserve this. You will be committing murder."

Van Horn did not answer. He wanted them to sweat.

When the nooses were finished, the Indians' hands were bound behind their backs, and the muscular Van Horn brothers hoisted them up onto their pintos, leading the horses under the huge limb of the cottonwood tree.

The hearts of Leaning Tree and Yellow Bird were obviously pounding in their breasts. The wind whipped Van Horn's silver hair around as he stood before them. In a crusty voice he said, "The Crow nation has needed a good example for years about trespassin' on white men's land. You two lyin' thieves are gonna be that example. It's time stinkin' red men learn that we whites are your masters, and we ain't gonna put up with your brazenness. Couple of corpses with stretched necks ought to get the message across."

Van Horn saw beads of sweat break out on the brows of the Crows in spite of the cold air. He was pleased.

Leaning Tree spoke solemnly. "Barth Van Horn, your sons not tell you I am son of Chief War Horse? There will be serious trouble if you kill me. Do not do this thing!"

Barth Van Horn threw back his head and laughed. Stepping up to Leaning Tree, he looped a noose over his head and cinched it tight on his neck. Then he took the second noose from Ben's hand, stepped over to Yellow Bird's horse, and with a flourish dropped the noose over the second Indian's head and jerked it tight.

The Crows gave each other a fearful look, and Leaning Tree spoke again. "Barth Van Horn, my father will come with vengeance!"

The big man laughed scornfully. "We white men will handle anything your father can throw at us!" With that he threw both ropes over the large limb overhead, saying,

"Clete, Jimmy, tie these ropes to that tree back there. Do it good so they won't slip. We don't want these red dogs to linger. We want their necks to snap as soon as the horses move."

Inside the house Holly and Sandra watched the scene from the kitchen window. Noticing that the ropes were not being anchored to the smaller tree, they realized that the whole thing was a trick on the Crows. Although they agreed it was a mean thing for the Van Horn men to do, they were relieved that the two Indians would not suffer bodily harm. Yet the prickling along Holly's spine, the premonition of disaster, would not leave her.

Clete and Jimmy made grunting noises as though they were tying the ropes securely to the smaller tree. "Okay, Pa," called Clete. "The ropes are tied."

Van Horn took one more look at the frightened young Crows, and then he walked behind their pintos, pulling off his belt. Doubling the narrow length of leather in his hand, he said, "Happy hunting, boys!"

The Van Horn brothers laughed hilariously when their father slapped the pintos' rumps with his belt. He hit Leaning Tree's horse first, sending it bolting ahead of the other. Leaning Tree's rope slid smoothly off the small tree and sailed free over the cottonwood's huge limb.

Instantly realizing that it was all a ruse, Leaning Tree turned to look back at his friend. What he saw hit his stomach like a battering ram.

Yellow Bird's rope had somehow tangled in the branches, and when his horse lunged at the sting of the belt, the rope went taut. Yellow Bird was yanked from the pinto's back as the noose snapped tight on his neck.

When Yellow Bird hit the ground and lay perfectly still, Leaning Tree knew something terrible had happened. His only choice was to ride to his village for help. Guiding his horse, he galloped south, the long rope trailing.

Barth Van Horn's heart was pounding as he looked down at Yellow Bird, whose head was cocked grotesquely to one side, a large lump at the base of his skull. He was still breathing, but his neck was broken.

Van Horn felt his insides tighten like drying rawhide. This joke had suddenly become horribly serious. The Crows would put on war paint over this, and the Van Horn farm would become a caldron of blood. His throat went tight. Wiping a shaky hand over his mouth, he raised his eyes to see if Leaning Tree was still in sight. The Indian and his horse were just disappearing into the forest.

Van Horn's voice was little more than a murmur as he said to his sons, "We don't dare let that Indian get to his village."

"You want me to get him, Pa?" asked Hale.

Nodding and swallowing hard, the elder man said, "Yeah. And take Clete with you. We can't afford any mistakes."

Hale and Clete leaped on their horses and galloped off.

Inside the house the women were equally stunned. Holly, still wearing her twin Colts under her jacket, said, "Sandra, keep Ma here." With that, she bolted through the door.

Rushing past her father and brothers, Holly knelt beside Yellow Bird. He was barely conscious, his lids fluttering over glassy eyes. The horrified young woman asked with trembling lips, "Yellow Bird, can you move?"

The young Crow could only give a small grunt in answer. Saliva ran freely from the corner of his mouth.

Holly stood up. Her angry eyes took in the faces of her brothers and the sagging features of her father. She walked over to Barth Van Horn and confronted him. "Pa, do you know what you have done? Why didn't you listen to me? Yellow Bird is paralyzed. His neck is broken."

Van Horn licked his lips but did not respond.

Wes spoke up. "Pa, what are we gonna do? When War Horse sees this, he'll massacre all of us!"

Van Horn licked his lips again and said, "War Horse ain't gonna see this. Hale and Clete will be back in a few minutes with the other one."

Holly's eyes bulged. "Pa, don't make it any worse than it is!"

"No choice now," the elder Van Horn said levelly. "We can't let War Horse find out about this."

Sam suddenly drew his revolver. "May as well go ahead and put this one out of his misery right now."

Holly looked at him in stark disbelief. "Sam!" she shrieked. "You're not going to shoot him?"

"Sure am." Grinning, Sam cocked back the hammer. "You heard what Pa said. The only way we can keep War Horse from findin' out about this is to kill them and bury them where he can't find them. It's as simple as that."

As Sam lowered the muzzle toward Yellow Bird's head, Holly lunged at him screaming, "No!"

Holly's hands closed on her brother's wrist, swinging the gun away from the paralyzed Indian. As Sam staggered slightly to keep his balance, the gun went off, the sound of the shot echoing sharply through the frosty valley. Holly screamed as her father fell. The bullet had hit him in the chest.

Dashing to him, Holly stared at the hole in his coat. Blood was already seeping all around it. As Van Horn gasped for breath, Holly cried out, "Pa! Don't worry. We'll get help for you."

Sam was half out of his mind. Wheeling about, eyes bulging wildly, he thumbed back the hammer of his smoking revolver and stood over Yellow Bird. He aimed the muzzle at the Indian's head. Yellow Bird stared fearfully, unable to move a muscle. There was a deafening roar; Yellow Bird's eyes saw no more.

Holly's head whipped around at the sound, and she knew what Sam had done. She bit down hard on her lower lip, and tears welled in her eyes.

No one had noticed Myrtle and Sandra on the porch until they heard Myrtle scream her husband's name. The frail woman pulled loose from Sandra's grasp and stumbled toward her fallen husband. Holly looked up as her mother collapsed, gasping for air and clutching her chest.

Holly snapped at her brothers, "Get Pa into a bed!" Then she and Sandra helped Myrtle to her feet and half carried her toward the house.

While Barth Van Horn was carried to the closest bedroom, the women laid Myrtle on the couch in the parlor. Holly said, "Sandra, get Ma's medicine into her. I'll check on Pa."

The frightened young woman ran to where Barth Van Horn lay on the bed, bleeding and gasping. Her brothers stood at the foot of the bed. Looking at the wounded man, she said, "I'll ride into town and get Doc Alton. Ma needs him too!"

Sam snapped, "No, you won't, Holly! If the doc is brought into this, there'll be no way to keep him from finding out what happened here."

"Sam is right, Holly," spoke up Ben. "Ma will be all right when she settles down, and we'll take care of Pa ourselves. Bringin' the doc here would be too dangerous."

"*Dangerous?*" Holly was exasperated. "You think Pa isn't already in danger? There's a bullet in his chest! He has to have the doctor!"

"Listen to me," said Wes, moving close to his sister. "There's a dead Crow Indian out there on the ground. Pa put the rope around his neck, and Sam put the bullet in his head. They'll both hang if anybody finds it out."

"Pa will die anyway without a doctor's care," Holly reasoned. "I'm going for Doc Alton."

Thinking of his own skin, Sam Van Horn grabbed Holly's arm and jerked her to him. His jaw jutted as he grunted, "You're not goin' anywhere."

A scowl crossed Holly's face. Surprising Sam with her quickness, she twisted from his grasp, took two steps back, and pulled her right-hand gun, thumbing back the hammer. Looking at Sam harshly, she issued a cold warning. "If you try to stop me, I'll shoot you. I mean it. And that goes for the rest of you too. Right now Ma and Pa are most important. They need Doc Alton, and I'm going to get him here."

The Van Horn brothers saw by the look in Holly's eyes that she meant business. She would not kill any of them, but she would make whoever tried to stop her wish he had been killed.

Dashing through the bedroom doorway, Holly called to Sandra to look after her father once Myrtle was calmed down. The sun was still high but the air was getting colder as Holly looked out the door. She jumped on her father's horse, which was still saddled, and then, casting a last look at the dead Indian, she galloped toward Billings.

The setting sun lighted the western sky in a fan shape as Holly Van Horn rode into town. She prayed that her father would be alive when she returned with the doctor. The bullet was close to his heart, and it had to have punctured a lung, but Van Horn had not been spitting up any blood. She also whispered a prayer for her mother.

Then the thought occurred to her that if Doc Alton knew how her father was shot, her brothers would want to kill the doctor to cover it up. She decided to tell him that her father's injury was caused by an accident. She hated lying, but there was no choice. Her parents needed Doc Alton, but she could not let the kindly doctor be killed while helping out. Gritting her teeth, Holly felt bitterness toward her father and brothers for what they had become. If Barth Van Horn had listened to her, this horrible thing would not have happened. It would have been better yet if Sam had let her send the Crows home before Van Horn had returned.

The lamplighter was lighting the wicks along Main Street as Holly galloped into Billings. Will Baker and Dusty Canfield happened to be looking out the window of the sheriff's office when she rode by.

"What's Holly doin' ridin' in by herself this time of day?" Dusty said aloud.

"I don't know, but I'll find out," Will Baker said, reaching for his coat.

The deputy stepped into the street in time to see Holly pull her horse to a stop in front of Dr. John Alton's office. She entered the office, and Baker decided to wait for her to come out. He pulled up his collar against the frigid night air.

Less than five minutes later Baker saw Holly emerge, followed by the doctor, carrying his black bag. Alton climbed into his buggy as Holly tied her lathered horse to the back of it. She pulled herself up next to the doctor, and they started down the street. As they drew near Baker he stepped into the street, waving his arms.

Alton reined to a halt.

"What's the problem?" asked the deputy, looking at both of them. He noticed the bruise on Holly's face.

"Barth's been shot," replied the doctor.

"What happened?"

"It was an accident, Will," volunteered Holly. "We've got to hurry. Pa's in bad shape." Feeling the guilt of the lie, Holly could not meet Baker's gaze.

Something in Holly's voice told Baker that he was not getting the full story. "You're not telling me everything, Holly. What is it?"

"Will," she said, a terrible sadness in her voice, "my ma's heart has gotten worse because of Pa's chest wound. I can't talk any longer. We've got to get to the ranch."

The deputy nodded silently and stepped back. He stood in the middle of the street and watched them until they disappeared from sight.

Chapter Five

The last rays of the setting sun were still visible on the western horizon when Will Baker and Dusty Canfield began putting on their coats at the sheriff's office in Billings. Matt London sat behind his desk. Leaning back in his chair, he stretched his muscular arms and said, "Don't you two boys lollygag at the café, okay? Get your supper down so I can go home to Amy."

Dusty clapped on his mangy hat and said to the deputy, "You know, Will, it's long been a mystery to me how this homely guy over here ever got such a beautiful woman to marry him."

Pulling on his fur-lined gloves, Will Baker grinned but said nothing.

Now buttoning his coat, Dusty deposited liquid tobacco in the spittoon and then said to the sheriff, "Matthew, you'd better count your lucky stars that Amy didn't lay those gorgeous eyes of hers on me first. She'd never have given you a second look!"

Laughing, London said, "Get out of here, you old fossil, or I'll make you spend the night in the cell next to Ruben Hatch."

"Let's go, Will," Dusty said, shaking his head as he moved toward the door. When he pulled it open, his eyes bulged at the sight before him. Chief War Horse and his son, Leaning Tree, were sliding from their horses' backs in the dim light of the dying day.

Over his shoulder Dusty said, "Matthew, we got company. It's War Horse and his boy. For them to show up at this time of day there's gotta be trouble."

The sheriff was already out of his chair and rounding the desk. He moved up to the door beside Dusty with his deputy pressing close. Stepping out into the cold, he smiled and said, "Hello, Chief. Evening, Leaning Tree."

War Horse stiffly acknowledged the sheriff's greeting. Leaning Tree did the same.

"We have serious problem, Matt London," said the chief. "My son and I talk with you."

After London ushered the two Indians through the door, Dusty closed it behind them and began peeling off his coat, with Baker following suit. Neither of them wanted to miss what the Crows had to say.

When the Indians were seated in front of the desk, London eased into his chair behind it. He had expected a visit from War Horse about the fight that morning between three of his braves and the Van Horns, but Leaning Tree's presence told him this concerned something else.

"Now, Chief," said the sheriff, "what's the problem?"

With a stolid face War Horse told London that he had planned to come the next day to talk with him about the Van Horns beating up his three braves, but now he had a greater grievance against the Van Horns.

The sheriff and his two men listened as together the chief and his son told of Leaning Tree and Yellow Bird's hunting excursion. Speaking in his somewhat broken English, War Horse told of the uproar in the Crow village when Leaning Tree rode in at a gallop with his hands tied behind him and the long rope trailing from his neck. The people wanted to know where Yellow Bird was, and when Leaning Tree told the story, the Crows were ready to arm themselves and go after the Van Horns to free Yellow Bird.

With his black eyes glittering the chief said, "I could restrain my people only because my son told them he and Yellow Bird were not actually hanged. However, Matt London, Yellow Bird *was* hurt."

Leaning Tree told the sheriff about seeing his friend yanked from his horse's back when the loose rope about his neck had somehow tangled in the branches. Knowing he could not help Yellow Bird, Leaning Tree had galloped on to the village. His last glimpse of Yellow Bird was to see him lying motionless on the ground.

"Do you think Yellow Bird was hurt seriously?" asked London.

"Not sure," replied Leaning Tree. "Perhaps breath knocked out of him."

"So you don't think the Van Horns were really planning to hang you and Yellow Bird?"

"No, Matt London," responded the young Indian, shaking his head. "They meant only to make us afraid. Something went wrong with Yellow Bird's rope."

War Horse said, "I do not believe life of Yellow Bird in danger. But wicked acts must be punished, Matt London! Instead of Crows punishing Van Horns, I have come to you to see it done. This is in keeping with pact between War Horse and Matt London."

The sheriff straightened in his chair and said softly, "I appreciate your doing so, Chief. As in the past, I assure you that justice will be done."

At that moment Will Baker said, "Matt, there's something going on with the Van Horns. Holly came riding in at dusk to fetch Doc Alton to the farm. I stopped them long enough to find out that Barth had been accidentally shot and was in bad shape."

London stood up from behind his desk. "Did Holly say how it happened?"

"No. She was in such a hurry, that's all I got."

London nodded, then looked at War Horse. "Chief," he said calmly, "if it is all right with you, I'll take Leaning Tree and go to the Van Horn farm."

"You not want War Horse to go?"

"I think it best if just your son and I go," London said evenly.

"Whatever Matt London decides sits well with War

Horse," agreed the Crow leader. "War Horse return to village."

"We will report to you as soon as possible," the sheriff told him.

Trusting the sheriff to rescue Yellow Bird and deal properly with the Van Horns, War Horse left the office and rode away into the night.

Baker and Dusty stood outside the sheriff's office as London and the young Crow mounted their horses. Pulling his fur collar up around his neck, the sheriff said, "Would you boys find someone to run over to my house and tell Amy not to look for me till she sees me coming?"

"Will do," Dusty answered.

"You two stay alert," warned the sheriff. "The Hatch gang could show up at any time."

"We'll stay on our toes," Baker assured him with a tight grin.

"You don't mind if we have some food brought in, do you, Matthew?" asked the old-timer.

"Just don't get too engrossed in eating," came the lawman's reply.

With a grin curving his lips Dusty countered, "I always eat with my eyes open, son."

As London turned his horse, he added, "By the way, it's time to stoke Hatch's stove. Take care of it, Dusty, will you?"

Dusty swore under his breath and spit tobacco juice into the street.

"What did you say?" asked London.

The old man gave him a wry look and replied, "I said I'd be happy to do it, Mr. Sheriff."

"That's what I thought you said." London grinned. He and Leaning Tree then headed eastward out of town and were soon swallowed by the darkness.

Holly stood in the dimly lit hall outside her father's room, in which Dr. John Alton was tending to his chest wound. Holly and the doctor had arrived minutes before, and now she was eager to hear the prognosis. Hale and Clete were with her, having long returned from their futile pursuit of Leaning Tree, and she could tell they were as concerned about what she had told the doctor about how their father was shot as they were about his welfare.

In a subdued voice Hale said, "What did you tell Doc, Holly?"

"Everything's fine, Hale. I want to check on Ma before—"

Hale grabbed her arm and pulled her around. "Ma's all right. Sandra's with her. Now tell me what you told Alton."

Jerking her arm loose, Holly said, "I told him the family was watching me do a new trick shot while riding, and that my horse stumbled just as I pulled the trigger. The bullet went wild and hit Pa in the chest. Does that suit you?"

As Holly was telling her tale her other brothers had walked into the hall and were listening. When she had finished, Hale gave her a crooked smile. "Good thinkin', Holly. I knew you wouldn't tell Doc Alton about the Indians."

The Van Horn brothers' relief showed in their eyes— especially Sam's, and he turned to Holly and said, "Little sister, I know you wouldn't let me and Pa hang."

Holly gave him a dull look, then turned to Hale and asked, "What would you have done if I had told the truth? Killed the doc to cover it up?"

"Yep," said Hale. "We sure couldn't let him blab that Pa put the rope on Yellow Bird's neck and Sam shot him in the head."

Holly's face flushed with anger. "I take it you didn't catch Leaning Tree, Hale."

"No. He reached his village before we even got close to him."

"What did you do with Yellow Bird's body? And his horse?"

"Buried the body in the barn floor," spoke up Wes. "Sam took the horse onto the reservation and turned it loose."

Holly's face filled with scorn. "Do you really think that's going to be the end of it? Don't you realize War Horse will come here with Leaning Tree? And probably a hundred angry warriors?"

"Them stupid Crows can't prove nothin', Holly," put in Ben. "Without a corpse they've got nothin' to pin on us."

"Yep," said Hale. "He got up, mounted his horse, and rode away. That was the last we seen of him."

"I hate what you all have become," Holly hissed. "Liars and killers!"

Sam grinned wickedly. "But you're part of the clan, little sister. You have to stand by us."

The young woman looked at her brother with fury and began to stride down the hall, saying, "I'm going to check on Ma."

At that moment Dr. Alton stuck his head out the doorway of her father's room. "Holly, I could use your help."

"Of course, Doctor," she replied, turning and heading back to assist the doctor in removing the bullet from her father's chest.

Holly and the doctor had been treating the elder Van Horn for over an hour when, from the kitchen, the brothers heard horses drawing up to the house. Hale jumped up and looked out the window. By the light from the lanterns outside he recognized Sheriff Matt London and Leaning Tree. Swearing, he pivoted and headed for the door.

"Who is it?" asked young Jimmy.

Hale told him and then added, "Wes and I will handle this. The rest of you stay in here."

The brothers, their eyes filled with trepidation, looked at each other as the door closed.

The eldest Van Horn sons felt the bite of the night air as they stepped onto the porch. The lawman and the young Crow were still astride their mounts as Hale asked in a voice as cold as the air, "What are you doin' here, Sheriff?"

"Business," came London's reply. "But first I'd like to know about your father. I understand he's been shot. I see Doc Alton's buggy is here."

"Accident," Hale said. "Doc's diggin' the bullet out of him right now."

Hale and Wes noticed Leaning Tree looking around the ring of light made by the lanterns.

"I'll get right to it," said London. "Leaning Tree told me about the hanging you had here this afternoon."

"Now, it wasn't a *real* hangin', Sheriff," spoke up Wes. "We was just teachin' those two Crow vermin not to trespass on our land. It's against the law, you know. *Federal* law."

"Leaning Tree told me why they were on your property."

Hale shook his head and snorted. "I'd expect a lyin' Indian to twist the truth, Sheriff. Look, it's a simple case of them two trespassin' on our land and shootin' our game. You ought to arrest them and lock them up."

Leaning Tree asked, "Where is Yellow Bird?"

Hale Van Horn could feel Matt London's eyes on him as he snapped, "How should I know?"

"Leaning Tree says his friend was lying on the ground when he rode away," said London.

"Yeah, he was. But except for a rope burn on his neck, he wasn't hurt. He got up like a scared rabbit, jumped on his horse, and rode off, headin' for his village. That's probably where he is right now."

"No," retorted Leaning Tree.

Hale's face was rigid. "Maybe he stopped off somewhere to get drunk. All I know is, he, was fine when he left here. I bet you anything he's in his tepee right now."

"He'd better be," warned London.

Without saying a word Leaning Tree slid from his horse, picked up one of the lanterns, and carried it to the spot where he had seen Yellow Bird fall.

"Hey!" blurted Hale. "Come back here with that!"

Ignoring him, Leaning Tree looked down at the frozen ground and called, "Matt London, come here!"

London swung out of his saddle. Hale and Wes followed him to where the young Crow knelt.

"Look," Leaning Tree said. "See blood on ground?"

As London bent down to examine the dark-brown spots in the dirt-encrusted snow, Hale said, "That's my pa's blood, Sheriff. He was standin' right there when the accident happened. That's right where he fell."

The lawman stood up. Looking at Hale, he asked, "Just how did this accident happen?"

"Well, we was all watchin' Holly do a new trick from the back of her horse this afternoon. She was, uh, shootin' at a tin can swingin' by a piece of string from that cottonwood over there. . . ."

As Matt London listened to Hale talk the lawman thought the story sounded farfetched, but he did not let on. "I'd like to speak with Holly," he finally said.

"You can't right now, Sheriff. She's helpin' Doc with the surgery."

"We'll wait," said London.

"Suit yourself," Hale said, walking toward the house. "C'mon, Wes, let's get inside. It's colder 'n blue blazes out here."

Leaning Tree carried the lantern and set it back on the porch. Turning to London as Hale and Wes disappeared through the door, he said, "If you alone, Van Horns would invite you inside . . . keep warm."

"I doubt it," London said glumly.

"Matt London," said the Crow, "I think they lie about Yellow Bird. I think Yellow Bird hurt . . . hurt bad. I think *his* blood on Van Horn soil, not Van Horn blood."

"I think they're lying too, Leaning Tree. Perhaps we'll know more after I talk to Holly."

Inside the house Dr. John Alton finished stitching up Barth Van Horn. When he and Holly emerged from the room, he told the family that their father had a good chance of making it, but it would be several days before he was out of danger. Then the physician entered Myrtle's bedroom, where Sandra waited with her.

Holly was surprised when Hale told her that the sheriff and Leaning Tree were outside and wanted to talk to her. But when he warned her to corroborate the story he and

Wes had told the sheriff, she fumed. She hated to lie, but she was backed into a corner. If Sam and her father were convicted of killing Yellow Bird, they would be hanged, and she could not let that happen. She also knew that the shock of such a thing would kill her mother. The only thing she could do was go along with her brothers' scheme.

Pulling on a heavy coat and a wool scarf that almost obscured her beauty, the young woman stepped outside. London and the Indian were stomping their feet and swinging their arms, trying to stay warm. Smiling to cover the tight feeling in her stomach, she said, "Sheriff, I'm sorry that you both have to stay out here. But there would be trouble if I invited the two of you in, and my mother couldn't stand any more of that right now."

"It's all right, miss," London assured her. "I just want to hear your version of what happened here today."

Holly quickly told him the same story that Hale and Wes had told, ending with Yellow Bird's riding off unhurt.

London then asked to speak with Sandra, and Myrtle, if she was able. Holly went inside.

A moment later Hale reappeared, wearing a heavy mackinaw. "Holly says you want to talk to Ma and Sandra," he said stiffly.

"I'd like to hear their versions of what happened here today."

"They didn't even see it," lied Hale. "Besides, Ma is too sick. And I think you've heard everything you need to."

London held Hale's gaze for a moment, and then he nodded and stepped off the porch toward his horse with Leaning Tree following suit. Swinging into the cold saddle, the sheriff said to Hale, "I'm going to the Crow village. If Yellow Bird isn't there, I'll be back here tomorrow."

Hale made no comment but bent to extinguish the lanterns and enter the house, where his brothers were all waiting in the kitchen, visibly upset.

"That lawman is gonna find out the truth as sure as shootin'," said Ben nervously.

"Nah," said Hale. "I keep tellin' you that without a body he can't prove a thing."

At that moment Dr. John Alton appeared, followed by Holly and Sandra. His face was grim. Running his eyes over the faces of Myrtle's six sons, he said, "Boys, you are going to have to keep things calm around here. Your mother is in bad shape. If she has any more upsets, her heart will fail. She'll die."

As Holly helped the elderly physician into his overcoat he said to the group, "I'll be back in a couple of days to check on your parents. Oh, and one of you will have to come into town tomorrow for more sedative. She has only enough to last her through the night."

"Thank you, Doctor," said Holly. "We'll be in to get it tomorrow."

Shifting his gaze between the two women, Dr. John Alton said, "You ladies take care of your father like I told you."

"We will," Sandra assured him.

The doctor climbed into his buggy and began the drive back to town, shaking his head in bewilderment. While he had been in Barth Van Horn's room he had seen the jacket that the bullet had passed through before striking the man's chest, and around the hole was a fuzzy black ring—powder burns. The doctor knew that powder burns resulted when a shot was fired at very close range, yet Holly and her brothers claimed that she had been more than thirty feet away when their father was hit.

How, the doctor wondered, could the family get a young woman like Holly to lie? And why?

Chapter Six

It was ten o'clock the next morning as Dusty Canfield stoked the small wood stove in the cellblock at the rear of the sheriff's office. He was alone there, except for the prisoner, Ruben Hatch, who stood watching the old man through the bars.

The outlaw's fiery hair and beard glinted even redder in the reflected glow from the opened door of the stove. His eyes had a wicked look. "My offer is still good, Deputy," Hatch grunted. "You let me out of here and you'll get five hundred dollars. Take a long time to spend that much money in this town, wouldn't it?"

Dusty piled in the last log, slammed the iron door, and adjusted the damper. He pivoted around on his good leg, shifted the plug of tobacco from one side of his mouth to the other, and then said caustically, "First off, I ain't no deputy; I just help out around here when Matthew needs me. What's more, you wouldn't give me no five hundred dollars if I *did* let you out. I've been around for a good many years, mister, and I know what you criminals are made of. And on top of that, even if I had an ironclad guarantee of a *million* dollars, I wouldn't let you out! You're goin' to the gallows because that's what you deserve. So shut up about me helpin' you escape."

Suddenly a tall muscular form appeared in the doorway that led to the office. "What's going on in here?" the sheriff asked.

Dusty ran a palm across his scrubby face and said, "Ruben keeps tryin' to bribe me to let him escape."

London shook his head. "Haven't you figured out yet that Dusty can't be bought, Hatch?"

The outlaw laughed. "Fact is, Sheriff, I don't need this worn-out old cuss to help me. My boys will be here anytime now to take care of that matter. They ain't gonna let me hang."

"You sound like Buford Way, Hatch." The sheriff grinned. "Ever hear about Buford?"

"This is gonna scare me, I suppose," Hatch murmured.

"Take it for what it's worth," said London. "It was just about two years ago. Way was like you—cocksure that he was going to be sprung from the very cell that you're standing in. To make a long story short, Will Baker and I were ready for Way's gang when they showed up. They're buried out in the cemetery. So's Way. He went to the gallows on schedule."

Ruben Hatch laughed hollowly. "It'll be different this time, London. You can bank on it. My boys ain't gonna let me go to no gallows! It'll be you and your deputy in the cemetery when this is over." Shifting his amber eyes to Dusty Canfield, he added, "And if this old coot is in the way, he'll get it too!"

Dusty's face turned beet red. "Old coot, huh?" he spit. "Go on back to the office, Matthew."

"What do you mean?" asked the sheriff.

"I mean go on back to the office!" blared the old man in his cracked voice.

London shrugged and then left.

Dusty limped to the stove. He looked over his shoulder at the outlaw, a crafty look in his eyes. "I'm gonna show you what happens to outlaws who call me an old cuss and an old coot." With that, he flipped the damper crosswise in the flue, stopping the flow of the smoke up the stovepipe. Immediately the room began to fill with smoke. Hobbling toward the door, he cackled, "Enjoy yourself, Hatch. This'll prepare you for where you're goin' in three days." Dusty could hear Hatch's coughing and swearing clearly even after he had closed the door.

Matt London looked up from his desk and grinned. "You're mean, aren't you?"

Dusty wiped tobacco juice from his lips. "I can get meaner."

"Just don't let the jail burn down."

"Don't worry, Matthew. Hatch won't get out of his hanging that easy." So saying, Dusty headed back into the smoky cellblock to open the flue.

The sun was approaching its highest point in the cold winter sky when Hale, Ben, and Holly Van Horn pulled into Billings in a wagon. After Ben drew the wagon to a stop in front of the general store, Hale helped Holly down and said, "You buy the supplies we need. Ben and I will carry them out to the wagon when you're done. Right now, we're goin' to the Big Sky for a few drinks and a card game or two."

"All right," she responded. "I'll meet you back here after I get the supplies and see Doc Alton for Ma's medicine."

Holly walked to the doctor's office. Upon entering, she greeted Dr. Alton and answered his questions about her parents. She felt vaguely uncomfortable with the man, having lied to him. While he prepared a bottle of the mild sedative Holly waited quietly. She was startled when the doctor suddenly said, "Holly, tell me again about your father's accident. How far from him were you when the gun went off?"

Trying hard to cover her nervousness, her brow puckered in concentration, she said, "About thirty . . . maybe thirty-five feet. Why?"

The physician looked away from her and mumbled, "As deep as the slug went, I would have sworn you were closer."

Holly's mouth dropped open and she looked at the doctor, but when he turned his eyes toward her, she quickly put the medicine into her handbag and said she must be going. Thanking the doctor for the sedative, she hurriedly left the office, wondering if Dr. Alton was really suspicious of her story or if she was just conscience-stricken because of her lies.

Though there was a hint of warmth in the sunshine that touched her face, Holly Van Horn was cold inside. She hated having to lie for Sam and her father for those two awful scenes, which were implanted indelibly in her mind: Barth Van Horn cinching the nooses on the Indians' necks . . . and Sam shooting Yellow Bird in the head.

But they were her family, and though she despised their ways, she did love them, and she knew she could never find it within herself to betray them by telling the truth. Even if she could, she knew that the shock and shame of her father's and Sam's hangings would kill her mother. Holly would then be indirectly responsible not only for her father's and brother's deaths, but also for her mother's. Her eyes filled with tears, which she tried unsuccessfully to blink away.

Looking up as she made her way along the street, Holly saw Alice Bryant emerge from the general store and head toward her. Alice and her husband, George, were neighboring farmers, and as the middle-aged woman came close her friendly smile turned to a look of concern. "Holly, dear," said the woman, "you're crying. What is the matter?"

With quivering lips Holly once again was forced to lie. She told Alice about the accident and about her mother's heart's acting up. The matronly woman embraced Holly against her considerable bulk, trying to give her words of encouragement.

Holly dabbed at her wet face with a hanky. "Thank you for your kindness, Alice. Oh, are Hale and Ben inside the store?"

"No, they're not, honey," responded Alice.

"Then they're still at the Big Sky," Holly said half to herself. "I'll have to go get them."

Alice Bryant's jaw slacked. With eyes wide she exclaimed, "Holly, you're not going to go inside the saloon!"

"Of course not! I'll stand in front of it until a man comes along who will go in for me."

"Heavens to Betsy! You frightened me, child!" gasped Alice, running a hand over her moon-shaped face. She sighed. "Well, I must be going. More shopping to do. Remember me to your mother. I do hope she'll be all right."

Holly noticed the conspicuous absence of anything said about her father—but then she could not blame Alice. Barth Van Horn's unpopularity was his own doing.

Walking to the saloon, Holly planted herself to one side of the door and waited for a man to approach the entrance. As she watched Alice Bryant move toward the dress shop a male voice from behind said suddenly, "Hello, Holly."

Wheeling about, she looked up into the face of Deputy Will Baker. She felt her face flush and her throat constrict. She thought of her father's command to stay away from the handsome young lawman and realized that Hale and Ben could come out of the saloon at any moment and see them standing there together.

While Holly was trying to find her voice Baker said, "Matt told me about your father's accident. I hope he'll be all right."

Holly was not sure whether her constricted throat was caused by fear of her father's finding out that she had talked to Will Baker or just by the man's nearness. Forcing out the words, she said, "Th-thank you, Will. Dr. Alton says Pa will be in danger for about a week."

While Holly fiddled with the collar of her coat the deputy said, "I . . . I've got to ask you this, Holly. I *have* to know. How do you feel about your father's insistence that we stay away from each other?"

Holly stood there battling her emotions. She was attracted to Will Baker—extremely so. She had even dreamed of being in his strong arms, sharing warm, tender kisses. Swallowing hard, she bit down on her lower lip and was about to answer when she spotted George Bryant coming up the street, obviously looking for his wife.

"Excuse me a moment, Will," she said, looking past him, thankful for the reprieve. "Mr. Bryant! Oh, Mr. Bryant! Are you looking for Alice?"

"Yes, I am, Holly," Bryant said as he hurried toward her. "Hello, Will."

Baker nodded as Holly said, "I think she might be in Hilda's."

"Thank you, Holly." The middle-aged man smiled and touched the brim of his hat.

Before he could move on, Holly said, "Would you do me a favor, Mr. Bryant? Would you go in the saloon here and tell my brothers that I'm ready to go home?"

"Gladly." Bryant nodded, pushing through the batwing doors.

Turning to the lawman, Holly said nervously, "Will, it would be best if my brothers don't find me talking to you."

"Is this the way you want it, Holly?"

Biting down on her lower lip again, she looked at him with misty blue eyes. "No, Will. It isn't. But—"

"Hale and Ben said to tell you they're still in a card game," interrupted George Bryant as he stepped back outside. "You are to browse around the shops and meet them at the general store in an hour." The farmer tipped his hat and walked off in search of his wife.

Will Baker cleared his throat and tried again. "You said that's not the way you want it?"

Wringing her gloved hands, Holly stammered, "Will, I . . . I am very fond of you. But . . . but if my father learns that I've been talking to you, he—"

"Is it the badge, Holly? Is my badge the problem?" Baker cut in.

She studied his face for a few seconds. "Yes, Will. Yes. It's the badge. My father has never favored lawmen, and now that he feels Sheriff London has denied him his reward money, he thinks even less of them. We'd have nothing but trouble from my father if we let something develop between us."

"Do you *want* something to develop between us?" Baker said softly.

Holly's eyes misted again. Without hesitation she answered, "Yes, Will, I do."

"So what your father is saying is that we could talk to each other if I didn't wear a badge."

She nodded sadly.

Grinning broadly, Baker unpinned the badge from his coat and slipped it into his pocket. "There," he said with a sigh, extending his arm for her to take. "Now we can talk."

Will Baker's charm and good looks totally overwhelmed Holly, and laughing, she said, "I guess we can!"

Holly's heart was pounding in her breast as she took his arm and they slowly walked down the street, their conversation warm and vibrant. Suddenly the deputy propelled her down a narrow alleyway, out of view from the street.

As they stood there looking into each other's eyes Baker said, "Holly . . ."

"Will . . ." she responded, her chest rising and falling with her rapid breaths.

A tingle traveled from the top of Baker's head all the way to his heels. "I . . . I'd like to kiss you."

"I'd like that too," she whispered back, her face tilted up to him, her mouth inviting.

Baker wrapped his arms around her, and as their lips came together Holly was free of worry over her mother and father for a few joyous moments. The shame that the Van Horn men had brought on the family, forcing her into a string of hated lies, was out of her mind while her lips meshed with Will Baker's in a sweet, lingering kiss.

They looked deep into each other's eyes for a moment and then kissed again. Holding each other close, Baker whispered into her ear, "No matter what happens, Holly, I won't let anything or anyone keep me away from you. What I feel for you is too strong, too deep."

A knot formed in Holly's stomach. She wondered how he would feel toward her if he knew she was protecting a brother who was a murderer and a father who might just as well be.

While Holly and the deputy were standing in the alley, six rough-looking men rode into Billings, dismounting opposite the sheriff's office. They tied their horses directly across from it in front of the tobacconist's shop, which George Bryant had entered while Alice browsed through the frocks at Hilda's Dress Emporium.

The leader of the six men was Tyrone Crisp, Ruben Hatch's right-hand man. As his followers quickly huddled together, Crisp nodded at two of them and said, pointing to the left of the sheriff's office, "You two, mosey around behind those shops and climb up on the roof. You know what to do."

Ed Butz and Joe Farner started casually walking toward the back of the buildings that stood to the left of the sheriff's office. Looking at Link Sutton and Don Tate, Crisp said, "Link and Don, you stay with me out here in front."

"Where do you want me, Tyrone?" asked Ray Carpenter.

"I want you up on the roof of the sheriff's office, Ray, just in case it gets rough down here. That way you, Ed, and Joe can put anybody on the street in a cross fire if you need to."

Carpenter nodded and headed across the street and toward the rear of the building, planning to climb up on the roof of the sheriff's office from behind.

Directly across the street Tyrone Crisp slowly lined himself up with the door of the lawman's office. He watched the townsfolk milling about in the sunshine, enjoying the small bit of warmth it provided. He waited patiently, giving his men plenty of time to get into place. He was also watching for the appropriate hostage to happen by. He preferred a woman.

Crisp looked up at the shops across the street, their tall wooden false fronts giving the impression of more substantial buildings. The building housing the sheriff's office and cellblock was the only one without a facade, and its roof was therefore clearly visible. Crisp saw no sign of Ray Carpenter yet, but then his eyes were drawn to the top of the false front on the building to the left. A black hat was being waved above it. He smiled, knowing the signal meant that Butz and Farner were in place.

Then, from the roof of the building to the right of the sheriff's office, he saw Ray Carpenter quickly lean out from behind the false front and nod. The outlaw leader laughed to himself at Carpenter's wise move—waiting to step over onto the exposed roof of the sheriff's office until the trouble had started.

Crisp noticed a young woman walking in his direction. If she kept coming, he would grab her as the hostage. He swore under his breath when she turned into a shop. But suddenly another woman was beside him, coming out of the dress shop. The outlaw waited until she closed the door, and then he seized the portly woman, who screamed as he jerked her into the street, the packages in her hands falling to the ground. Crisp whipped out his gun, cocked it, and pressed the muzzle to the woman's head. She continued to scream.

Roughly clamping her neck in the crook of his left arm, the outlaw said, "Shut up, lady, or I'll kill you right now!"

The woman's mouth shut in fear. Her eyes were wild, and she released a tiny whimper.

At that moment George Bryant ran out of the tobacco shop, shouting, "Hey, you! Let go of my wife!"

"Back off, mister," bellowed Crisp, "or I'll blow her brains all over this town!"

"Now, look here!" blared Bryant. "You let go of Alice!"

Link Sutton stepped up onto the boardwalk behind Bryant and struck the man's head with the butt of his revolver. Bryant slumped to the boardwalk and lay still. Alice started to scream again but stopped herself when Crisp prodded her with the pistol.

At Alice's first scream Will Baker and Holly Van Horn had run from the alleyway where they had sequestered themselves. Holly gasped as her eyes fixed on the outlaw holding Alice a hundred feet down the street. Other people on the street had frozen where they were standing.

"Holly, you stay here," Baker insisted, moving toward the scene. Holly, however, followed on his heels.

As the deputy moved along he saw that it was Ruben Hatch's gang, come to break their leader out of jail and spare him the gallows. Baker's eyes darted back and forth across the dusty street, and in addition to the man holding Alice Bryant—the one he knew as Crisp—he spotted two others, Sutton and Tate, also standing across from the sheriff's office, their guns drawn. Baker figured there had to be more gang members somewhere.

He kept walking slowly. He knew that without his badge he would probably be mistaken for some citizen who had decided to be brave.

Then Crisp spied him and shouted, "You there! Stop right now! Take one more step and I'll kill her!"

Baker heard Alice moan loudly, as if her whole body was trembling. The deputy stopped.

Inside the sheriff's office Matt London and Dusty Canfield had not yet heard a thing, Ruben Hatch's coughing from the smoke-filled cellblock and his stream of profanity having drowned out all other noise. But then a deep, bellowing voice from outside shouted, "Hey, Sheriff! Come out here! I want to talk to you!"

"Hatch's gang," said Dusty.

London eased up to the window, careful not to be too visible, and looked across the street.

Dusty swore when London said, "It's Tyrone Crisp. He's got Alice Bryant." Like his deputy, London could not see any gang members other than the two who flanked Crisp. He let his eyes roam the area, but only townspeople were in view, standing like statues—except for George Bryant's crumpled form, still lying on the boardwalk.

London then saw his deputy standing some thirty feet up the street to Crisp's left. Will Baker had not yet drawn his gun, and London saw that he had had the presence of mind to remove the badge from his coat. As far as the outlaws knew, Baker was just one of the bystanders, afraid to raise his gun against them.

The seasoned sheriff knew that Baker was wisely waiting for his boss to make his move. Then the deputy would go into action.

Word had spread along the street that something was happening. One man ran into the Big Sky Saloon, and within seconds the patrons were craning their necks over the swinging doors to see what was going on. Among the curious onlookers were Hale and Ben Van Horn, who must have seen their sister standing a few feet behind Will Baker.

Still peering through the office window, Matt London eyed the sun, which was nearing the apex of its arc. Because of the overhang of the roof, the interior of the sheriff's office was deep in shadow, and movement inside would be hard to see from where the outlaws stood across the street.

London left the window and pulled a Winchester .44 from the gun rack. Levering a cartridge into the chamber, he headed for the door.

"What you gonna do, Matthew?" Dusty asked softly.

"I'm going to see if I can take that guy's head off," came the dry reply.

Tyrone Crisp's voice bellowed across the street again. "Hey, Sheriff! I want to talk to you! Get out here right now or there's gonna be blood in the street!"

London put his hand on the doorknob. Speaking over his shoulder, he said, "Dusty, you stay in here. Whatever happens, don't let anybody get in this office!"

The old man already had his shotgun in hand. Patting the barrels, he said, "Don't worry, Matthew. Fanny May and I can cover things."

London swung open the door and took two steps back, keeping himself in the shadow.

Out on the street Will Baker tensed when he saw the

door of the sheriff's office open. Aware that Holly stood only inches behind him, he whispered, "Holly, get away. Bullets are going to fly, and I don't want you to get hit."

Holly took one step back then halted. She did not want to move far from Baker.

When the office door swung open, Tyrone Crisp tightened his grip on Alice Bryant's neck, pressed the barrel of his revolver snug against her head, and shouted, "Show yourself, London!"

"Speak your piece!" called the sheriff, remaining out of sight.

"Release Hatch this minute!"

Alice wailed frightfully and sagged, her weight pulling the outlaw with her. For two or three seconds the muzzle came away from her head as Crisp jerked her upright.

Matt London took note of it. Being an excellent marksman, he knew that with the muzzle away from Alice's head all he needed was a clear shot at two inches of the outlaw's face.

"Send Ruben out right now," blared Crisp. "Or else this woman dies!"

London shouted back, "Let her go, Crisp. Hatch stays where he is."

Alice's knees sagged again, and Crisp's gun came away from her head long enough for him to hoist her back up in front of him. This time Matt London shouldered his Winchester and drew a bead just to the right of Alice's ear.

"Sheriff!" shouted Crisp, trying in vain to make out London's form in the shadowed door. "I'm givin' you thirty seconds! If Hatch don't come through the door by then, I'm blowin' this woman's head off!"

Alice wailed in fear, and London held the rifle steady, waiting for her to sag again.

Will Baker eased his coat back, giving his hand free access to the gun on his hip. He could hear Holly's measured breathing a few feet behind him. Again he whispered to her to move away.

People on the street stood with bated breath. Inside the

saloon the Van Horn brothers watched with both interest and fear.

Alice Bryant took a deep breath and wailed again, her knees buckling. Her weight pulled Crisp off balance and the revolver came away from her head.

Matt London's rifle roared instantly, bucking in his hands, and Tyrone Crisp's right eye disappeared, his blood spraying the boardwalk. The outlaw's gun fired harmlessly, but the noise roared in Alice's right ear, and she screamed repeatedly as Crisp fell, twitching like a beheaded chicken.

Link Sutton and Don Tate raised their revolvers to fire into the darkness of the doorway, but London, who had already fed another cartridge into the chamber, fired at Tate. The bullet drilled the outlaw's chest, the impact of the blast laying him out flat on his back.

At the same instant, Will Baker drew his revolver and shot Sutton before the outlaw could fire.

As London moved out onto the boardwalk Will Baker saw two heads pop up on the roof next to the sheriff's office, both men aiming at Matt London. Raising his revolver again, Baker shouted, "Matt! Look out!"

The warning saved London, but it drew attention to the deputy, and one of the men on the roof, Joe Farner, fired off a shot that grazed Baker's head. The other, Ed Butz, fired at the sheriff, but London had ducked back into the doorway, and the bullet punched through the boardwalk instead.

When Baker went down, Holly scooped up the gun that had fallen from his hand and shot at Farner just as he was about to fire his second shot. The bullet ripped through his neck, and his body nosedived off the building and cracked hard as it hit the boardwalk.

At that instant Matt London drew a bead on Ed Butz and fired. Butz stiffened from the impact and then fell backward onto the flat roof.

Concerned about his deputy, London reloaded his rifle and waited for several minutes to be certain that still another outlaw was not hiding. Then he made his way cautiously toward the three fallen outlaws across from his office, wanting to be sure they were indeed dead. He knelt by one and felt for a pulse, then began to move on toward another. At that moment he heard a shrill whistle from across the street and, looking toward his office, saw Dusty Canfield standing in the doorway, pointing upward with one hand and holding his shotgun in the other. In the same instant the sheriff took in a figure on the roof.

London aimed and fired his rifle in one smooth motion, the shot transforming Carpenter's startled face into a mass of blood. The sheriff looked at Dusty and smiled in appreciation.

Crouching in the quiet street, London waited a moment to be sure yet another member of Ruben Hatch's gang was not waiting to surprise him. He saw Dusty disappear into the darkness of the office and figured the old-timer was checking on the prisoner. The sheriff cautiously rose and moved toward Will Baker, whose head was already being cradled by Holly. She was using a handkerchief to dab at the trickle of blood that ran down his temple.

The Van Horn brothers dashed to their sister before London had reached her and the deputy. Meanwhile George Bryant had regained consciousness and was sitting beside his weeping wife, speaking softly, attempting to comfort her.

When Matt London got to his fallen deputy, he was relieved to learn that Baker had only been stunned by the bullet that had grazed his head, and he had witnessed Holly's grabbing his gun and killing Joe Farner. Baker looked up weakly when he saw London standing above him.

"You all right, Will?" the sheriff asked.

"I am now," Baker said with a grin as he looked up at Holly.

"You know, I wouldn't be standing here if you hadn't let me know those two were up on the roof," London said. "Thank you, Will. I owe you."

"You don't owe me anything," the deputy said. "It was the least I could do after everything you've taught me."

Limping up to the knot of people, Dusty Canfield spit a stream of tobacco juice and said, "Glad to see you're in good hands, Will." The old-timer cackled.

Matt London put an arm around Dusty's shoulder and said, "Thanks for whistling when you did, friend. How'd you know from inside that Hatch's man was up on the roof?"

Dusty spit again. "Because he had to be the loudest, most clumsy son of a gun that ever walked!"

After everyone had stopped laughing, London said, "Dusty, go in and tell our friend Ruben that he's still going to the gallows as scheduled."

"With pleasure!" the old-timer said. "He'll be fit to be tied."

London smiled down at Holly. "Thank you for jumping in to help. That was some shooting."

"Sure was," Baker agreed. "That second shot might have ended it for me."

Holly blushed as Baker looked at her tenderly. With a warm smile she said to London, "You didn't do too bad yourself, Sheriff. I'll bet Alice can still hear the whistle of that bullet!"

"That reminds me. I'd better check on her. I'll be back in a minute, Will," London told him.

As the sheriff walked away Baker said, "Let me see if I can get on my feet."

Holly helped him up, and he stood swaying, his arm around her neck. She steadied him by holding his waist.

The two Van Horn brothers stepped up to them, Hale glowering at his sister as Ben said, "You ought to be ashamed of yourself, Holly! Poor Pa lyin' on his bed, tryin' to stay alive, and you here in town playin' up to the very man he told you to stay away from. Pa's gonna be madder'n a stuck hog when he finds out. Wouldn't be surprised if he has a relapse."

"Don't be meddlesome, Ben," she snapped. "And I

won't let go of Will until he can stand on his own." She
was on the verge of blurting out that she was in love with
Will Baker, but then she decided it was best kept secret
for the time being.

"Tell me, did this dirty lawman lay a hand on you,
Holly?" Hale said.

At that, Will Baker started toward Ben, but Holly leaped
between them. "No, Will! Don't fight with them. I'll go
on home, and you get over to Doc Alton. Let him tend to
your wound. I'll see you later."

"You will *not* see him later, Holly," blurted Hale.

The young woman's voice reverberated off the wooden
walls. "Stay out of it, Hale! If I want to see Will again, I'll
see him again."

Both brothers were about to respond when the tall
figure of Matt London appeared. The brothers bit back
their words when London growled, "You two get on your
horses and ride . . . right now! There's been enough grief
here for one day. I don't want any more."

"Look who's talkin' about grief!" Ben sneered. "You
sure didn't mind takin' a chance with Mrs. Bryant's life,
did you, London?"

Looking at the younger Van Horn coldly, London said,
"Ben, if I had had any doubt about where that bullet was
going, I wouldn't have fired. And besides, no outlaw is
ever going to intimidate me and break a prisoner out of
my jail."

Hale Van Horn's face blossomed red. With a wicked
rasp in his voice he pointed a stiff finger at the sheriff and
said, "I owe you one, lawman."

Matt London's muscles shook with petulance as he
growled at Hale, "If you want another beating, I'll be glad
to oblige."

Without further comment the Van Horn brothers took
their sister by the arm and headed up the street toward
their wagon. Holly looked back and gazed softly at the
deputy, the look in her eyes telling him that they would
indeed see each other again.

Chapter Seven

As Hale, Ben, and Holly Van Horn rode out of Billings, Dusty Canfield hobbled back to the sheriff's office and made a beeline for the cellblock. He entered and found Ruben Hatch standing at the bars, gripping them hard. Dusty noted the dread etched on Hatch's florid face, which seemed to darken as he saw the old man grinning.

"Well, Ruben, your boys gave it a good try." Dusty laughed dryly.

The outlaw leader's lips moved for a few seconds before his voice came. Finally he croaked, "They all dead?"

"Yep. All six of 'em. But don't let it get you down. Couple more days and you'll be joinin' 'em!"

Ruben Hatch's knees appeared to be about to give way beneath him. Without another word he turned and slowly made his way to the bunk in the cell's corner. Easing down on it, he lay on his side, drew his knees up, and wept.

Dusty returned to the office, cackling.

When the lawmen entered Dr. Alton's office, with London steadying the injured deputy, the doctor was in the final stages of setting a young boy's broken arm in a cast. Nearby was the boy's mother, sitting on a straight-backed chair and watching the physician work.

Looking up, his hands wet with plaster of paris, Alton asked, "What was all the shooting about, Matt? I was setting this boy's bone when the ruckus broke out, and I couldn't leave him to see what was going on." Then his eyes moved to the deputy and saw the bloody handkerchief that Baker still had clutched to his head. Motioning to a chair in the far corner of the room, he said, "Sit down, Will. I'll be with you shortly."

London helped his deputy to the chair, then said, "It was Ruben Hatch's gang, Doc."

Putting the finishing touches on the cast, Alton asked, "You were expecting them, weren't you?"

"Yep."

"Since you and Will are alive and kicking, I assume you won the battle."

"Yep. Thanks to Holly Van Horn and Dusty Canfield."

"Holly? What did she do?"

"Saved Will's life by killing one of the outlaws who had him dead-centered."

Alton gave an approving nod. Then speaking to the boy, he said, "There you are, Bobby. Stay off barn roofs from now on, okay?" The physician gave the boy's mother a few instructions on the care of the patient, and the two of them left.

Washing the plaster from his hands, Alton instructed the deputy to sit on the examining table. Then he went to work on the head wound. While he dressed it, he asked the sheriff, "Anybody out there on the street need my attention, Matt?"

"Not unless you're an undertaker," London replied evenly.

"How many of them were there?"

"Six."

The doctor shook his head. "I heard a woman screaming."

"Alice Bryant. One of the gang grabbed her and put a gun to her head. She was pretty scared."

"How'd you get her away from him?"

"I waited till I had a clear shot. Then I blew his head off."

Baker winced as pure iodine touched the raw wound.

The physician worked silently for a few moments as he dabbed alcohol around the edges of the wound. Finally he said, "Matt, I was going to come over and talk to you about Barth Van Horn."

The sheriff kept watching Alton work. "Oh? What about him?"

"They're trying to cover something up by saying that Holly accidentally shot him. It might have been an accident, but it didn't happen the way she told me it did."

The sheriff's brow furrowed. "Why do you say that?"

Pressing a thick piece of gauze to the wound, Alton said to his patient, "Hold that right there, Will." Then he stepped to his medicine cabinet and took out a large roll of bandage and a pair of scissors, saying, "Holly told me she shot Barth from a distance of thirty or thirty-five feet, from the back of her horse."

Matt London took hold of the straight-backed chair and spun it around, sitting down in it backward. His eyes never left the aging doctor's face.

Alton returned to his patient and continued, "The bullet I dug out of Barth's chest was shot from below the wound. The bullet's path definitely angled upward, though it was a slight angle. If Holly had shot him from her horse, it would have been angling downward." The doctor started wrapping a bandage around Baker's head.

"Did you ask the Van Horns about it?" asked the sheriff.

"Nope. I haven't let on that I know Holly's lying. And there's more. When I was alone in the bedroom with Barth, I got a look at the sheepskin coat he was wearing when he got shot. It was lying at the foot of the bed. There were powder burns on it. You don't get powder burns at thirty feet."

Matt London sighed. "I wonder if Barth's shooting might be linked to the incident that took place with Leaning Tree and Yellow Bird."

"Well, it isn't like Holly to lie," put in Alton. "For her to do that, she must be backed into some kind of a corner."

"Protecting her father and brothers from the gallows would be enough to put her in a corner, wouldn't it?" said London. He shook his head and then added, "I'm more sure than ever that Yellow Bird is dead."

"What are you going to do about it, Matt?" asked Baker.

"I should be hearing from War Horse sometime today. If Yellow Bird still hasn't shown up, I'm heading to the Van Horn farm for some answers."

It was midafternoon when Dusty Canfield, crossing the main room of the sheriff's office to reach the spittoon, noticed the approach of four riders. Peering through the window for a better look, he recognized them as Chief War Horse, Leaning Tree, and two other Crow braves. The dark eyes of the Crow chief reflected his dire concern as the Indians reined in at the sheriff's office and dismounted under the cloudy sky.

The old-timer turned to the sheriff, who sat at his desk, and said, "Matthew, War Horse is here. He's got his son and two others with him—but no Yellow Bird."

Will Baker was seated in a chair with its back leaned against the wall, but both he and London stood up as Dusty hobbled to the door and opened it for the visitors.

The Indians stepped into the office; one look at War Horse's morbid expression told the story.

"Welcome, Chief," said London, working up a smile.

War Horse set his black eyes on the sheriff and spoke in a dismal monotone. "Sometime in the night the pinto of Yellow Bird returned without him, Matt London. My people have searched reservation all morning. Yellow Bird not to be found."

London ran his fingers through his thick curly hair. "I don't like the sound of this, Chief."

"Van Horns not telling truth. War Horse think rope on neck of Yellow Bird killed him. If this is so, Matt London, there will be much trouble."

London pulled at his ear nervously. "Chief, if the Van Horns have killed Yellow Bird, I guarantee you they will be punished to the fullest extent of the law. I'll ride out there now and look into the matter."

A scowl whipped across War Horse's face. "These braves will go with you."

Looking the chief square in the eye, London said, "It is best if I go alone, War Horse. I ask you to allow me to handle this myself."

The Indian was quiet for a moment. Then he said reluctantly, "War Horse will do what you ask, Matt London."

"I'll let you know what I find out as soon as I leave the Van Horn place," London assured him.

The chief nodded woodenly and led his men outside. Silently mounting up, they rode away.

When Dusty had closed the door, Will Baker said, "Matt, I want to go with you. If the Van Horns *have* done something to Yellow Bird, you could be in real danger by yourself."

Matt London pulled his revolver, broke the action, and spun the cylinder, checking the loads. Flipping it back in its holster, he looked at his deputy slyly. "Are you sure you're worried about my being in danger, or are you just wanting to see Holly?" Then in a more serious tone he said, "If we have to arrest her father or some of her brothers, Holly just might put an end to her friendship with you, my boy. Are you ready for that?"

Baker shook his head, disagreeing. "Holly wouldn't do that, Matt. She doesn't go along with her brothers and father. She proved that when she risked her life to save mine by shooting that outlaw."

"Can't argue with that." The sheriff smiled.

"So I'm going out there with you," said Baker, ending the conversation.

"What do you mean you were just walkin' down the street with him?" Barth Van Horn, in spite of his weakened condition, had found the strength to rail at his daughter. "I told you to stay away from him!"

The entire family was gathered in Barth Van Horn's

bedroom. Myrtle was seated in an overstuffed chair near the bed, while Sandra stood protectively next to her and the elder brothers were positioned in a half-circle. Jimmy stood in the doorway.

From her father's bedside Holly shot Hale a venomous look and then said to her father, "I was going to tell you about it myself when the time was right, Pa. I knew you'd get angry, and I didn't want to upset you—and of course I didn't want to upset Ma."

"Well, Hale did right in tellin' me," growled the Van Horn patriarch. "What I say around here goes, young lady!"

"As long as Hale told you this much, Pa," spoke up Ben, "you might just as well hear the rest of it. Holly mixed herself up in a shoot-out with Ruben Hatch's gang and killed one of 'em. She did it to save Baker's miserable neck."

The huge man's face grew red. Glaring at Holly, he said slowly, "You saved a stinkin' lawman's life at the risk of your own?"

Holly looked over at the drawn, ashen face of her mother. Myrtle's cheeks were sunken, and there were dark circles around her eyes.

Looking back at her father, she said, "Couldn't we talk about this alone? This isn't helping Ma."

"You should have thought about your mother when you disobeyed me, girl!" Van Horn thundered. "We're gonna talk about it right now. You have shamed this family."

"Pa, listen to me. I—"

"You are never to go near that tin star again, Holly. I mean it."

Setting her jaw, Holly glowered back at her father in an audacious, steely manner. She knew she had fallen in love with the handsome young deputy, and drawing strength from this newfound love, she decided that she was going to stand up to her father for the first time in her life. Clenching her fists at her sides, she declared, "Pa, don't talk to me about shaming the family. Or about protecting

Ma—after all, Sandra and I do all the caring for her. Listen to me, Pa. I have a right to see whom I please. And since I think a great deal of Will Baker, I will see him all I want." Her words snapped crisply, coming faster. "This is your house, so you can throw me out if you want to, but you are not going to stop me. And neither are the rest of you," she said to her brothers as she whirled and faced them in their half-circle. "Just try it."

The whole family remained stone-cold silent.

Holly looked at her father and continued, "If you tell me to leave, Pa, I'll go. But I'm warning you—I'll take Ma with me. And Sandra, if she wants to go. I wouldn't be one bit surprised if she did!"

Barth Van Horn sat nonplussed, looking as if he was in shock. His anger had drained his strength, and Holly's brashness totally bewildered him. Never had his authority been defied so brazenly by a member of his family; he was completely at a loss as to how to handle it.

In a ploy to gain sympathy from the other members of the family, he began gasping for breath, wheezing out that his chest wound was stabbing him with pain. Holly dropped to her knees beside his bed and took hold of his hand, but he wrenched it from her.

Tears spilled down her cheeks as she said, "Pa, I love you. I never wanted to hurt you or cause you grief. But I can't go along with you anymore. Your hatred for lawmen has nothing to do with your believing they're all hypocrites who bend the law to suit themselves. You don't like lawmen because they pose a threat to you and my brothers—because of what you've become!"

Holly took a deep breath. Her father only stared at her, so she continued, "You haven't told the rest of us what you had to do to rob the stagecoach—or how much money you got from it. Did you have to shoot somebody, Pa? Has it gone that far now?"

Still there was silence. Clete and Wes cast furtive glances at Hale's granite face.

Proceeding, Holly said, "Pa, I don't know why you've

let my brothers become monsters, but I hate it! I hate what happened here with that poor Indian boy. And none of you seem to have any conscience about it at all! I'm ashamed of all of you, and I think Ma and Sandra feel the same way!"

Clete shot a quick glance at his wife, and Sandra gave him a cold stare. In the doorway Jimmy Van Horn shifted nervously on his feet, his head bowed, while Myrtle sat quietly weeping. Barth Van Horn just stared straight ahead, his jaw clenched stubbornly. He refused to answer.

Whipping her head around, Sandra said to Hale and Ben in a scathing tone, "Why did you have to open your big mouths about Holly and Will?"

Lashing back, Ben said, "Pa had a right to know, Sandra! Hale and I did what we had to."

Sandra looked to her husband for help, but Clete merely looked at her dispassionately.

Then Sam said curtly, "Who do you think you are, Sandra? You keep your nose out of this family's business!"

Standing up to meet Sam's scornful gaze, Sandra tossed her long dark hair and retorted, "I'm part of this family, and I've a right to speak my piece!"

"You're part of this family by marriage—nothing more," said Sam, stepping close to her. "Since Clete made the mistake of marryin' you, that's *his* problem. But you ain't got no say in family matters!"

Sandra trembled with anger. Giving a short contemptuous sniff, she said, "Clete's real problem is having you for a brother!"

Sam slapped Sandra's face violently, and she staggered backward into the wall. Putting a hand to her stinging cheek, she looked again to her husband for help, but none came. Instead, he looked at her with impassive eyes and said, "Sam's right, Sandra. Since by blood you ain't a Van Horn, you ought to keep your mouth shut."

Fury ignited in Sandra's breast as she said heatedly, "You're a sorry excuse for a husband!"

Sam grinned at his brother. "You're okay as a husband, Clete. You just got the wrong wife."

Her anger getting the better of her, Sandra slapped Sam as hard as she could.

Swearing at his wife, Clete grabbed her by the shoulders and began shaking her savagely. "You shouldn't have done that to my brother, Sandra!" he bellowed.

"Stop . . . stop it! *Stop it!*" Myrtle screamed.

Clete let go of Sandra abruptly, and Holly dashed to her mother.

Sam fixed his sister-in-law with a venomous glare. "You better stay out of my way, woman, or I'll kill you!"

For a moment the two just stood, glaring at each other. Then Sandra said, "Listen to the big, brave man! He's going to kill a woman half his size!"

From behind her, Hale's deep voice bit like a whip. "Get out of this room, Sandra, before I throw you out!"

Sandra's long black hair swirled as she turned to face the eldest brother. Baring her teeth, she said hotly, "And here's another big, brave man! He's so tough, he can throw a hundred-pound woman out of a room!"

Hale took a step in her direction, but he froze when his father called, "Hale! Leave her alone!"

Sandra's eyes glared at her husband. She then darted through the door past Jimmy, her footfalls thumping down the hall, followed by her bedroom door's slamming.

Holly helped her weeping mother from the chair. "Come," she said soothingly, "I'll help you to your room. It's time to take your sedative."

Silence prevailed as Holly assisted her mother through the door. The Van Horn men stared at one another, finding nothing to say.

After an hour had passed, things had quieted down at the Van Horn house, and some normalcy was returning. Jimmy, on the back porch stacking firewood, was stepping off the porch to get another armload when his attention was drawn to movement out on the prairie. By squinting he could just make out the familiar forms of Yellowstone County's two lawmen. Pivoting, he ran into the house.

"Hale!" called the gangling youth, charging through the kitchen.

The eldest brother emerged from his father's bedroom, meeting Jimmy in the hallway. "What is it, kid?"

"The sheriff and his deputy are comin'!"

Within seconds the Van Horn brothers had gathered in the kitchen and were looking out the frosted windows. As the two riders drew near, Hale said, "Put your coats on, boys, and we'll all go out to meet 'em. But let me do the talkin', okay?"

While the six Van Horn brothers were putting on their jackets and hats, Holly came into the kitchen. "Did I hear Jimmy say the sheriff and deputy are coming?" she asked.

"Yeah." Hale nodded, moving toward the door. "Are you gonna let your feelin's for that deputy cloud your thinkin'?"

"What do you mean?" she asked, squaring her shoulders.

"I mean, are you gonna stick by our story, or are you gonna break and tell the truth?"

Holly felt the weight of her deception. But swallowing hard, she said huskily, "I'll stick with the story. I don't want Pa and Sam to hang. For Ma's sake especially."

Pointing a stiff finger at Holly, Hale warned, "Stay in the house." With that, he opened the door, and the brothers filed outside.

Chapter Eight

Sandra Van Horn paced back and forth in her bedroom, seething with anger toward her spineless husband and his bully brothers and trying to decide what to do. Barth Van Horn and his sons were criminals and should be made to pay for their crimes.

She had no idea how long she had been pacing when she heard Jimmy's excited voice in the hallway. Some of his words were indistinct, but she got the idea that someone unwanted was coming. Her bedroom was at the rear of the house, and by angling herself just right at her window, she could view the back porch. When she saw that the unwanted visitors were the sheriff and his deputy, she opened the window slightly so she could hear the conversation between the lawmen and the Van Horn brothers.

Stepping in front of his brothers, Hale adjusted his hat and looked up at the mounted lawmen. He looked directly at Sheriff Matt London and said in an unfriendly tone, "What do you want this time, London?"

"Yellow Bird's pinto returned to the Crow village last night, but he wasn't on it," came the reply.

The big man spread his legs apart in a defiant stance. "That's too bad. So why'd you come here?"

"This is the last place he was seen alive. I want to talk to your father."

Bristling, Hale replied, "Pa's too weak to talk."

London's horse snorted and stamped as if in response to the sheriff's thoughts.

Will Baker was scrutinizing the faces of the other five brothers, wondering if this confrontation was going to result in a shoot-out. He prayed that it would not. As bad as Holly's brothers were, he did not want to shoot any of them. He noted, however, that all but Jimmy were wearing guns.

"What is it you're wantin' to know?" Hale asked London brusquely.

"It's what I want to *see*," London replied with tight lips.

"See?"

"Yeah. I want to see the coat Barth was wearing when he was shot."

Hale regarded the sheriff incredulously. "What do you want with Pa's coat? What does it have to do with your missin' Indian?"

"Maybe a whole lot," responded the sheriff.

"Well, we ain't got it. The bullet hole ruined it, so we burned it."

London knew Hale was lying, but he also knew that getting the Van Horns to hand over the coat could be a problem. "Burned it, eh?" he said, looking the big blond man square in the eye. "You sure must've been in a hurry to get rid of it."

"Why should we be in a hurry?" asked Hale.

Spacing his words deliberately, the sheriff replied, "Because the powder burns on it prove that Holly's story of how Barth got shot is a lie."

Hale narrowed his pale blue eyes. "Are you sayin' my sister is a liar?"

The other brothers tensed.

"Whoever forced her to tell that story is the real liar," came London's blunt reply.

Hale Van Horn felt a chill run down his spine. None of the family had even noticed the powder burns. He wondered how the sheriff could possibly know. Deciding that London must be bluffing, Hale began to feel more confident. He laughed hollowly and said, "And how would you know if the coat had powder burns on it?"

"Doc Alton told me. He saw the coat in your father's room."

The chill on Hale's spine now clutched it with icy fingers. Obviously unnerved, he retorted, "What would powder burns prove anyhow?"

"That Holly did not shoot your father from thirty-odd feet away. But that's only part of it. He can tell by the angle of the wound that the shot wasn't made from a horse either."

Hale fought to maintain his composure. Clearing his throat nervously, he said, "Doc is wrong. The story Holly told him is true."

Adjusting himself in his saddle, the sheriff spoke in a level voice. "Doc is not wrong, Hale. He knows what he's talking about. I guarantee you, his testimony will stand up in—"

Sandra Van Horn bolted through the back door, cutting off London's words. In her hands was a sheepskin coat.

Shouldering her way past the surprised men, Sandra stepped off the porch and held up the coat for London's inspection. Her face was defiant as she said, "I've been listening from my window, Sheriff. Hale is lying, as you can see for yourself."

Will Baker's nerves tightened. His senses were honed, ready for trouble if it came.

The sheriff took the coat and examined it. A four-inch circle around the bullet hole was flecked with black powder. He showed it to Hale, and the man's face blanched.

"Please don't blame Holly, Sheriff," said Sandra. "They forced her to tell that ridiculous story."

"Shut up, Sandra!" roared Hale, fixing her with a menacing glare.

"I will not!" she snapped back. "I'm telling the whole story right now!"

Hale Van Horn panicked. He clawed for his gun, and his four armed brothers followed suit. But before any of them could clear their holsters, they faced the ominous muzzles of the lawmen's guns. To a man they froze in place.

"Everybody just stay calm," London said slowly. "Now raise your hands as high as you can reach them. My deputy is going to take your weapons."

Faces grim, the Van Horn brothers lifted their hands. Will Baker dismounted and took their revolvers while London held them at gunpoint. The sheriff noticed that Sam looked suddenly ill. As Baker carried the collection of revolvers over to the toolshed and deposited them on a bench inside, Sandra pulled her plaid wool shawl tighter around her. London could not tell whether her shaking was from the cold or fear.

London slid down from his horse and draped Barth Van Horn's coat over Sandra's shoulders. Then he ordered the Van Horn brothers to sit on the porch. Again he noted how pale Sam looked.

With his deputy standing beside him London said, "All right, Sandra, tell me the whole story."

Under the burning eyes of her husband and brothers-in-law, the pretty brunette told how she, along with Myrtle and Holly, had watched the entire hanging incident from inside the house. She said Barth Van Horn was the one who had come up with the idea in the first place and that Myrtle and Holly had begged him to let the Indians go free.

The lawmen listened intently as Sandra explained how Barth Van Horn was shot when Holly was attempting to save Yellow Bird's life, and how Sam killed the young Crow by shooting him in the head. She finished by saying, "If you want Yellow Bird's body, Sheriff, you'll find it buried in the floor of the barn."

"Thank you, Sandra," the sheriff said with a tight smile. "Now everything falls right into place." He ran his gaze over the faces of the brothers and asked, "Any of you going to deny that Sandra has told me the truth?"

There was no answer. Clete, Sam, and Hale regarded the small woman malevolently.

Facing Sam, London said, "Stand up. I'm arresting you for the murder of Yellow Bird."

The guilty man offered no resistance as London handcuffed him to one of the heavy posts that held up the porch roof. Sam's face was chalk-white.

"Keep them all right here," London said to his deputy. "I'm going in for Barth."

"You can't take Pa to jail, Sheriff," blurted Wes. "He's in bad shape."

Ignoring him, London turned to the young woman and said, "Sandra, you come inside with me."

When Matt London ushered Sandra inside the house, he found Holly standing near the window in the kitchen. "I have to arrest your father, Holly," London told her.

"I know." She nodded glumly and led London into Barth Van Horn's room.

Myrtle was sitting close to her husband's bed in the overstuffed chair, and she watched his face closely when the sheriff confronted him with the truth.

"I'm arresting you for the murder of Yellow Bird, Barth," London stated in a flat voice.

The old man glared at the sheriff but said nothing.

Myrtle began weeping. The sheriff turned to her and said, "Mrs. Van Horn, I know you're in poor health, but I have no choice. I have to do this."

"I know, Sheriff," the aging woman said softly, sniffling.

Holly and Sandra flanked Myrtle, their hands reassuringly on her shoulders. Holly looked at London and said, "Sheriff, I hated lying to you and Doc Alton . . . and to Will. You have to understand that—"

"I understand fully, miss," London cut in. "I'm sure we all would have done the same thing if we'd been put in your position."

Tears brimmed in her eyes. "Thank you," she breathed.

Sandra bent her head to her mother-in-law. "I'm going

to have to leave here, Ma. I can't stay with Clete hating me now."

Myrtle's weeping intensified as she reached up and pulled Sandra down to embrace her.

Holly turned to London and said, "Sheriff, can't you let my father stay here until he's feeling better?"

Barth Van Horn broke his silence. "Yeah, Sheriff. I can't ride into town. I'm in pretty bad shape."

"I'd say Yellow Bird is in *worse* shape, wouldn't you?" London snapped coldly.

Looking at Holly, London said, "I'm sorry, miss, but he's got to go to jail with Sam. Your brothers would try to scoot him off somewhere to escape the law. Don't worry, Doc Alton can care for him in the jail—and we'll borrow one of your wagons to take him there. He'll be comfortable enough while waiting for his trial."

Barth Van Horn suddenly broke into a blustering string of profanity. His face flushed and angry, he roared, "All of this is so stupid! Killin' a dirty Indian shouldn't be no crime. Somebody ought to pin a medal on me and Sam for what we did."

London forced himself not to shout back. "Yellow Bird had as much right to live as you. Since you and Sam ignored that right, you must pay." He paused, then added, "You'd better get dressed. It's cold outside."

London turned on his heels and left the room. He had just stepped out on the porch when he heard Hale say angrily to Baker, "You two will never get Pa and Sam to town. We'll see to that!"

Slamming the door hard behind him, London got everybody's attention. He glared at Hale, saying, "You'd best forget whatever you have planned, mister! Chief War Horse is expecting us to stop by the Crow village on our way back. If we don't show up there, he'll bring his warriors *here*."

Hale's face blanched.

"And if any of you are thinking about doing me in later," continued the sheriff, "you'd better think again.

When War Horse learns who murdered Yellow Bird, I'll be the only man who can keep him from coming here with a war party, taking your scalps, and burning this place to the ground! You'd better hope I don't die from either natural or unnatural causes anytime soon."

The Van Horn brothers looked at each other in frustration. There was no way they could withstand an attack from the Crows.

London said to the lanky boy, "Jimmy, will you hitch up a team to one of your wagons? And if you want your pa to be comfortable, lay something soft in it."

Jimmy nodded and headed toward the corral.

At that moment Holly stepped out on the porch, her eyes brightening when she saw the deputy. Crossing to where he stood with Matt London, she said, "Will, I hope you can forgive me for deceiving you."

Since the sheriff was standing nearby and could keep her brothers covered, Baker holstered his gun. He reached for Holly's hands and held them tightly. With a warm smile he said softly, "I forgive you one hundred percent." Baker drew Holly into his arms. Looking over the top of her blond head, he saw that London was grinning with pleasure. He also noted the look of contempt in the eyes of her brothers, causing him to suggest, "Holly, maybe you'd better come into town. You might not be safe here."

"They won't hurt me, Will. And with Sandra's leaving, I really have to stay to care for my mother." Smiling, she rubbed his shoulders where her hands rested on them and said, "Don't worry, I'll be all right."

At that moment Jimmy drove up with the wagon, and while Sam and Barth Van Horn were being helped into it Sandra appeared on the porch, dressed in her Sunday coat and hat. Looking at London, she said, "Sheriff, would you mind if I rode into town with you?"

"Not at all, ma'am," he responded. London knew that Sandra was in danger if she stayed on the farm, having revealed the murder. "You can ride with Will. He's going to drive the wagon."

"I'll be glad to drive, Sheriff. That way Mr. Baker can ride his horse."

London nodded and then asked, "Aren't you taking anything with you?"

"There isn't time to pack anything. Holly can bring my belongings to me later."

"Do you have somewhere to stay in town?"

"No, sir. But I'll figure out something."

Throwing the Van Horn brothers a sharp look, London said, "You can stay at my house, ma'am. My wife and I will be glad to have you."

Sandra managed a smile. "Thank you, Sheriff. I appreciate it. I won't stay long—maybe a night or two. I'll work something else out by then."

The lawmen mounted up, and as London settled in his saddle he said to the Van Horns, "You boys better pray that I can keep War Horse from going on the warpath."

When Sandra clucked to the horses, the wagon lurched sharply, Sam Van Horn swaying with the movement. He looked down at his father, who was lying flat on his back with his eyes closed, and he wondered if the man felt as scared as he did. His heart was pounding so violently that the blood beating in his ears was like thundering drums.

When the lawmen and the wagon had traveled from view, Wes Van Horn swore and said, "Let's mount up and go after 'em. Let's get Pa and Sam back right now!"

"Don't panic, Wes," said Hale, trying to maintain calm in his own voice. "London wasn't kidding. He's the only one who can keep War Horse from comin' after us. We'll bust Pa and Sam out of that jail later, after he talks to the chief."

"You mean like Ruben Hatch was busted outta there today?" Ben said sarcastically.

"We gotta stop 'em now!" Wes insisted. "Once the Crows hear the truth about Yellow Bird's death, who's to say what'll happen?"

Clete added, "Yeah, let's dig up the body and bury it elsewhere."

"Too late for that," Hale snapped. "The smart thing to do is leave things alone—for the time being."

"Right now," put in Jimmy, "I think we ought to go in and see to Ma. She needs us."

The boys filed into the bedroom where their mother still sat in the overstuffed chair. They pointedly ignored Holly, who sat at her feet speaking words of comfort. Myrtle was sobbing inconsolably.

While all the attention was fixed on their mother, Wes slipped out unnoticed. Tiptoeing through the house, he put on his hat and coat, grabbed a rifle, and quietly went outside. Running to the toolshed, he retrieved his revolver and then dashed to the barn and saddled his horse. He rode at a walk for fifty yards so as not to draw attention, and then he put the horse into a fast gallop.

The lawmen and their charges were within two miles of the Crow village when Sam said to London, who was riding beside the wagon, "You could be takin' us into a death trap, Sheriff. Do you realize that?"

"What are you talking about?" London asked.

"War Horse might just decide to take us away from you and kill us on the spot. I'd feel better about it if you'd take us to town and put us in the jail before you tell him."

"Don't fret, Sam," the sheriff said from the side of his mouth. "War Horse and I are friends. He won't do anything like that. You'll be hung nice and legal."

When Barth Van Horn moaned, Sandra looked over her shoulder, concern written on her face. "Are you hurting bad, Pa?"

The man set hard eyes on her and growled, "What do you care, traitor?"

Sandra bit down on her lower lip and straightened in the seat.

London heard Van Horn's bitter words and felt his temperature rise. "Listen, Barth," he hissed, "it's not her fault you're in this fix. She didn't put the ropes on those Indians' necks."

At that instant a rifle cracked from behind a clump of bushes off to the right, the sound echoing across the snow-covered Montana prairie. The bullet buzzed past London's head. As both lawmen drew and fired into the bush, another bullet sang past the sheriff's right ear. Both men fired again.

There was a bellow of pain as Wes Van Horn rose up and staggered from behind the bush, two bullet holes showing in his light-colored coat. As he raised his rifle to fire again, hatred burned in his face, and an animallike growl came from his mouth. London and Baker fired again, their shots sounding as one. The slugs punched into Wes's chest, and his rifle discharged harmlessly as he spun slowly on one heel and then crumpled, dead.

Sam Van Horn was up on his knees in the back of the wagon. Shaking his handcuffed fists at the lawmen as they laid Wes's body in the wagon beside his father's, he railed, "You dirty killers! You could have tried to take him alive. You didn't even give him a chance."

Matt London eyed him with disdain and said flatly, "Shut up."

When the party finally reached the Crow village, Sam sat close to his father and trembled with fear as hundreds of Indians gathered in a large circle around the wagon while Matt London told War Horse the whole story. Sandra stood between the two lawmen, not eager to stray from their protection.

As the Crow chief listened, his face was as stolid as carved wood—except for his eyes, which were aflame with anger. When London finished, War Horse spoke with deathly calm. "Matt London must ride away and let Crow have these men!"

Holding his voice steady, London said, "You know I can't do that, War Horse. These men are under my jurisdiction. They are my prisoners. But you have my solemn oath: They will face trial, and justice will be done."

After a few seconds in which the furious chief seemed to be fighting his emotions, he said, "War Horse can attend the trial?"

"Certainly."

Satisfied that London would keep his word, War Horse asked that Yellow Bird's body be brought back for proper ceremonial burial. The sheriff promised him it would be done the next day.

A few hours later—after the Van Horns were locked up and Dr. John Alton had been brought in to check on Barth, and after four men had been hired to exhume Yellow Bird's body the next morning—the sheriff took Sandra back to his house and explained the situation to Amy. The two women liked each other immediately. Seeing them together, London noticed the resemblance between the two dark-haired women.

Amy, smiling warmly, said, "We have a spare bedroom, Sandra, and it's yours as long as you need it. I'm so sorry that things have turned out so badly for you. If you need a shoulder to cry on, I have that too."

Tears welled in Sandra's eyes. "Thank you, Mrs. London. I have no family, but I'll find a place to stay as soon as I can, so as not to wear out my welcome here."

"You won't do that, Sandra," Amy assured her. "And since we're your family for at least a little while, please call me Amy."

"All right, Amy," she said, brushing away a tear. "Thank you."

Looking around, Amy asked, "Did you bring your belongings? Your clothes?"

Sandra explained the situation.

"Well, until Holly brings them," replied Amy, looking her up and down, "you can wear some of my clothes. We seem to be just about the same size."

It was midmorning the next day when Hale and Ben Van Horn rode into Billings under a threatening sky and dismounted in front of the sheriff's office. Shouldering their way through the door, they found Matt London and Dusty Canfield sitting in the office.

"We want to see Pa and Sam," Hale said, not bothering to keep the bitterness out of his voice.

London nodded, relieving them of their gun belts and hanging them on wooden pegs next to the gun rack. While doing so he told them the circuit judge was due in Billings in three days. The trial would be held then.

"We're also lookin' for Wes, Sheriff," said Ben, a little more evenly. "He rode off the farm yesterday not botherin' to tell anybody where he was goin'. We figured he went to town to get drunk and that he'd be home by dawn. But we've checked the drinkin' places, and nobody's seen him. I don't suppose you have either."

London drew a deep breath and said grimly, "Yes, I saw him. Yesterday afternoon. I was just now getting ready to ride out to your place, boys, to give you the news. I'm sorry to have to tell you this, but Wes is dead. He tried to bushwhack Will and me, and we had to kill him. His body is over at the undertaker's. If you want to, you can take him home for burial. The undertaker is waiting to hear from you. Your pa and Sam were in no condition to make decisions last night, and I haven't talked to them about it this morning."

Sullen and saddened, Hale and Ben entered the cellblock alone, and the four Van Horns commiserated about Wes's death and their sorry state of affairs. Barth Van Horn allowed as to how ironic it was that he was feeling somewhat better.

Looking through the bars, Hale said, "Pa, don't you worry none. We're not gonna let you hang. We'll bust you and Sam out of here."

Ruben Hatch spoke up from his cell. "You'd better plan it well and be real careful. London, Baker, and that old geezer out there wiped out my gang."

"Well, it ain't gonna be so easy for London and his two sidekicks this time," said Hale. "They're facin' Van Horns.

When the smoke clears, it'll be the tin stars who are buried."

Hatch remembered saying virtually the same thing. But all he said now was, "How about makin' a break before tomorrow mornin'? I'd sure like to go with you, but I'm supposed to hang at sunrise."

The outlaw was ignored.

After a few more words of reassurance to their kin, Hale and Ben left the jail and went to the undertaking parlor. There, they placed Wes's body in the wagon that had brought it into town the day before and headed home.

Chapter Nine

Suspecting an attempt of some kind to break Sam and Barth Van Horn out of jail, Sheriff Matt London hired eight townsmen to stand guard day and night. Dusty Canfield was among them.

London left the eight men to keep watch while he prepared for the hanging of Ruben Hatch. The gallows was constructed on wooden skids and stored behind the jail. When it was needed, the upright framework was pulled into the center of the main street and placed directly in front of the sheriff's office. As he oversaw the placement of the gallows the sheriff talked with one of the townsmen about the procedure.

When the time for the hanging drew near the next morning, a large crowd was in attendance, and among the many spectators were Hale, Clete, Ben, and Jimmy Van Horn. They had been trying to devise a plan to rescue their brother and father and were disheartened to see London's army of men guarding his office.

The crowd quieted down as the sheriff's office door opened and Matt London appeared, leading the handcuffed prisoner. Behind them were Will Baker and Dusty Canfield. The guards in front of the building parted when the sheriff and Ruben Hatch approached, and beyond them the crowd—among them the Van Horn brothers—followed suit. All eyes were on the unhappy face of Ruben Hatch, who briefly scanned the crowd as if searching for

someone to help him. But then he cast his eyes downward, continuing his walk to the gallows.

The sound of whispering washed through the crowd as
Hatch slowly climbed the stairs, followed by the deputy.
When they were on the platform, Will Baker put the black
hood over the man's head and looped the noose over it to
his neck. Having tightened the noose, Baker then stepped
back.

All eyes turned to where Matt London was standing,
ready to pull the lever. He waited for a few moments, and
the only sound that could be heard was Ruben Hatch's
muted sobbing.

Then it happened, and Hatch suddenly dropped to the
end of the rope.

The Van Horn brothers turned away as the minutes
passed and Hatch's body was taken from the gallows. Then
Jimmy spoke to his oldest brother. "Hale, what're we
going to do? I counted eight men around the outside of
the sheriff's office. There may be more inside. How can
we ever save Pa and Sam?"

"I don't know yet, little brother," Hale said, shaking his
head. "But there has to be a way."

As the now-empty gallows was pushed on its skids back
behind the jail, each of the Van Horns stared after it. They
all hoped they could come up with a plan to prevent the
ominous wooden structure from being pulled to the center
of town once again in just a few days' time.

Two days later the Van Horn trial was held at the
Yellowstone County Courthouse. The eight guards formed
a circle around the two handcuffed prisoners as they were
led one block from the jail to the courthouse. No one was
allowed in the courtroom until the prisoners were in their
places at a table to the left of the judge's bench. Dr. John
Alton watched closely as Barth Van Horn sat down at the
table, noting that the man was still quite pale and drawn.
The prisoners were flanked at the table by the sheriff and
his deputy.

The men London had hired confiscated gun belts and rifles at the door. Only they and the two lawmen were allowed to carry weapons inside the courtroom.

The entire Van Horn family attended the trial, including the weak and feeble Myrtle. When she entered the courtroom, supported by Holly and Jimmy, and laid eyes on her husband and son, she began to weep. She and the other family members seated themselves on a long bench in the first row, directly behind Barth and Sam Van Horn.

Sandra Van Horn was there to testify. She was also seated in the first row, across the aisle from the family, with Amy London beside her. Clete leaned forward, caught his wife's eye, and gave her a poisonous look, which Sandra returned.

Sheriff Matt London twisted in his chair beside the prisoners and looked over the crowd that was gathering in the courtroom. Then he saw War Horse enter, followed by Leaning Tree and four other Crow braves. They took seats in the back row. The sheriff and the chief locked glances momentarily, and War Horse nodded but did not smile.

Matt London felt the weight of the chief's glance. He knew that War Horse was expecting a verdict of guilty, and he was confident that the jurors, who had been selected the day before but had not yet appeared, would convict Barth and Sam Van Horn of Yellow Bird's murder. Judge Hiram Southard would then certainly sentence them to the gallows. If by some quirk they were acquitted—or even if they were convicted but only got a prison sentence—there would be big trouble with the Crows.

London let his eyes stray to a nearby window. Dark clouds hung low, as they had the last few days—a sure sign that a healthy snowstorm was at hand. He hoped bad weather was all that was imminent. Just then the jury of twelve men filed in, their faces somber. As soon as they had taken their seats, Judge Hiram Southard came in and sat down, and the trial was under way. The atmosphere in the courtroom was tense as Southard called for evidence against the two accused men. London testified that the four men who had exhumed Yellow Bird's body had found rope burns on his neck and a bullet in his head. Then each of those men corroborated the sheriff's statement. Sandra Van Horn was called to the stand to give her eyewitness account of the incident, and when she had finished, the jury retired to make their decision.

While the jury was out, Hale Van Horn looked across the aisle and caught Sandra's eye. *I'm gonna get you!* he mouthed at her, causing the brunette's blood to run cold.

The jury returned in ten minutes with the verdict. Both Barth and Sam Van Horn were found guilty of murder.

The sheriff breathed a sigh of relief, then waited apprehensively for the sentencing as the Van Horn family sat in numb silence. At the back of the courtroom the Indians watched with piercing eyes as Barth and Sam Van Horn rose to hear the judge proclaim their sentences. When the sheriff saw the elder man faltering, he leaped up and helped him stand. Sam's face was colorless.

Judge Hiram Southard, a thin man of sixty, tilted his head down and looked over the glasses low on his nose. "Sam Van Horn, you have been found guilty of murder by the jury of this court. Do you have anything to say before sentence is pronounced?"

Sam mumbled, "I was just tryin' to put the Indian out of his misery. His neck was broken. He'd have been paralyzed the rest of his life—and he probably wouldn't have lived too much longer anyway."

"You were not dealing with an animal, Mr. Van Horn," the judge said curtly. "You had no right to take his life." With a firm voice Southard then declared, "You are hereby sentenced to hang by the neck until dead. The execution will take place tomorrow morning at sunrise."

Sam looked dazed.

Setting his hard gaze on the older man, the judge said, "Barth Van Horn, you have been found guilty of murder by the jury of this court. Do you have anything to say before sentence is pronounced?"

The big man cleared his throat to find his voice. "I didn't shoot the Indian. The rope I put on his neck didn't kill him. And Sam was only bein' merciful when he shot him."

Judge Southard was not going to hash over the details again. "Is that all you have to say, Mr. Van Horn?"

"Yeah." Van Horn nodded, leaning on the lawman.

"Barth Van Horn," said Southard, "you are hereby sentenced to hang by the neck until dead. Because of your weakened physical condition, said execution will take place one week from today at sunrise."

As the judge's gavel came down on the desk to dismiss the court, Myrtle Van Horn gave a loud gasp and collapsed on the floor. Dr. John Alton jumped up and pushed his way through the crowd, kneeling beside her. After checking Myrtle's pulse and pulling back her eyelids, he reached out and tenderly put his hand on Holly's shoulder. Holly, holding her mother's right hand, was weeping. "I'm afraid she's gone," the doctor said.

The Van Horn brothers pressed close, looking into their mother's pallid face. The physician looked up at them and said somberly, "Her heart gave out. She's dead."

Holly cried out, covering her mouth, and Jimmy put his arm around her. While Clete and Ben looked at each other helplessly, fury spilled through Hale, blind rage taking control of him. Bending over, he pulled up a pantleg and reached down into his boot, producing a double-barreled derringer.

Behind the bench Judge Southard had risen. Matt London, still standing at Barth Van Horn's side, caught sight of the derringer in Hale's hand just as he pointed it at the judge and fired.

Several voices in the crowded courtroom screamed out as Judge Southard stumbled backward from the impact of the slug. He hit the wall, clutching his chest and gasping before closing his eyes and sliding down to the floor.

A wisp of smoke rose from one barrel of the derringer as

Hale swung it around and aimed at Sandra. Her eyes bulging, she began backing up—right into Amy London.

London dove onto Hale a second before the shot was fired. The slug shattered a window as the two men sailed across the floor, slamming into several chairs.

London raised up on one knee, braced himself, and chopped Hale on the jaw with a stinging blow. The big Dutchman flopped flat on the floor. The sheriff shouted for his deputy to get some men to take Hale, Sam, and Barth Van Horn to the jail, and while the three were being ushered out under heavy guard, London ran behind the judge's bench.

Dr. Alton had left Myrtle Van Horn in order to tend to Judge Southard, but it was no use. The judge was dead.

The sheriff, wiping the sweat from his brow, walked over to where Holly still knelt over her mother's lifeless body. Sandra and Amy were trying to comfort her. Ben, Clete, and Jimmy huddled close, speechless at the sudden calamity.

"I'm so sorry this happened, miss," London said to Holly. Looking up at the three brothers, he said, "I'm going to have someone get the undertaker."

Ben's nostrils flared as he replied coldly, "The Van Horns take care of their own. Ma will be buried beside Wes on the farm."

London nodded and walked away.

Clete Van Horn was standing over Sandra, who was kneeling beside her grieving sister-in-law. Glaring at his wife, he growled, "This is all your fault, Sandra. If you hadn't opened your mouth, the law could never have proved that Pa and Sam killed the dirty redskin!"

Upon hearing the words the brunette burned with anger. "It was your pa's hatred for Indians and his fool stubbornness that brought all this on. Don't be blaming me for it!"

Clete was raising a fist to strike her when a hand clamped down on his shoulder. "Don't do it, Clete," Matt London said. "Take your mother and go on home."

Clete Van Horn's bulky form seemed to slump as he lowered his hand. With a hateful look at Sandra he turned to his brothers and said, "I reckon we'd better go."

While Holly talked with Sandra and Amy, her brothers lifted their mother's body, carried her out of the courthouse, and laid her in the wagon. Gripping the side of it, young Jimmy said, "Hale is gonna hang for killin' the judge, ain't he?"

Ben closed the tailgate firmly. "Hale ain't gonna hang—and neither are Pa and Sam. We're gonna get 'em out of there." Looking over his shoulder to make sure no one was close enough to hear, Ben said quietly to Clete, "You know the dynamite we bought for blowin' the tree stumps out of the alfalfa field?"

"The dynamite in the toolshed? Yeah." Clete's eyes widened. "Ben, we can't blow up the jail with Pa and the boys inside! It would kill 'em!"

Ben saw Deputy Will Baker and the other men who had taken the prisoners to jail come from the sheriff's office and head in their direction. Lowering his voice even more, Ben said, "We ain't gonna blow up the jail. I've got somethin' better in mind. Now hush up."

At that moment Matt London and Dr. Alton emerged from the courthouse, followed by the three women. Ignoring the hateful stares of her brothers, Holly embraced Sandra, telling her that she loved her. She then turned to Amy London and thanked her for giving Sandra shelter.

Putting an arm around Sandra, Amy said to Holly, "She's welcome in our home as long as she wants to stay."

Holly managed a smile, then said to Sandra, "I'm sorry I haven't gotten your belongings to you yet."

Sandra patted Holly's hand. "Don't worry about it. Amy has been kind enough to keep me clothed."

When Holly turned toward the wagon where her three brothers waited, she suddenly found herself looking at Will Baker. The deputy laid his hands on her shoulders and said softly, "I am truly sorry about your mother. If there is anything I can do, please let me know."

Holly reached up and touched his strong hand, her eyes filming with tears. "Thank you, Will," she said in a half-whisper. "You're doing it right now. You're giving me strength."

When Ben and Clete began speaking at once, loudly telling Baker to get away from their sister, Holly turned on her brothers with heated scorn. "You two mind your own business!"

Ben lashed back, "Pa told him to stay away from you, and I intend to see that order carried out!"

Holly drew in a deep breath to retaliate, but Will Baker stopped her. Squeezing her shoulder, he said, "Let's not press the issue now, Holly. Everyone is upset because of what's happened here. Let's wait until all of you get over your mother's death."

"You ain't gettin' any closer to her when our grievin' is done with, mister," Ben snarled.

"When I want to see her again," Baker said firmly, "the likes of you won't stop me!"

Enraged, Clete stepped up, seized Holly by the arm, and jerked her away from where Baker, now flanked by Matt London, stood. "Get in the wagon!" he commanded.

A sudden wildness raced through the deputy. With the quickness of a cougar he sank his fingers in the bulky man's coat and spun him around. Then he cracked him with a solid punch to the jaw, and Clete went down.

Ben started to move in, but he froze when he heard the double click of a shotgun. Dusty Canfield was standing behind him.

A wicked gap-toothed grin on his face, Dusty spit in the street and waggled a finger at Ben while shaking his head. Ben took two steps away from the deputy, all the while eyeing Dusty's shotgun.

Clete struggled to his feet. His eyes were glazed, and he was unable to focus. He heard the deputy say, "You keep your hands off her, Clete. Being her brother doesn't give you the right to manhandle her."

Shaking his head and blinking to clear the haze from his

eyes, Clete grunted, "You ain't a part of this family, tin star. Butt out!" Then he took a swing at the fuzzy form in front of him.

Baker easily dodged the big meaty fist and slammed three quick punches to the husky man's jaw. Clete staggered, swung again, and met a crushing blow that popped like a flat rock dropping into mud. The Dutchman went down on his back, and Baker stood over him, a rugged shape against the gray sky. "Clete!" he barked. "If I ever find out you've touched a hair on Holly's head, I'll pound you to a pulp!"

Clete watched the deputy help Holly onto the wagon seat. Then he spotted his wife. Sandra Van Horn was smiling, looking as if she had enjoyed the show. When she saw his eyes on her, she shook her head and turned away.

Clete rolled to his knees, attempting to stop the world from whirling. As he tried to get up his brothers moved to his side, helping him up and into the back of the wagon. Jimmy climbed in beside him, and they both stared with frozen hearts at the draped body of their mother.

While Ben was climbing into the seat Holly leaned over and kissed Will Baker on the lips. "I love you," she whispered.

Angrily Ben snapped the reins and the wagon bolted away.

Matt London, standing next to his wife, watched the wagon disappear down the street. Then he noticed War Horse and his braves, who were standing by their horses down the street and waiting to talk to him. Turning to Amy, London said, "Honey, you and Sandra go on home now. I'll see you later."

London approached War Horse, who greeted him with a friendly smile. The chief expressed his appreciation for seeing to it that Yellow Bird's killers had faced the law and were consequently going to hang. Then he and his braves mounted up, saying they would be back for the hangings.

As the Indians rode away, Matt London looked back to

where Dusty Canfield and Will Baker were left standing alone. He waved to them and walked toward his office.

Waving back, Dusty Canfield spit a brown stream and said to Will Baker with a sigh, "Sure looks like I'm in danger of losing my five bucks. That young Van Horn gal seems to have taken a shine to you."

Baker grinned at the old-timer and said, "I think you ought to pay up right now."

Dusty cackled and shook his head. "You ain't done no formal wooin' yet!"

"You saw her kiss me, didn't you?"

"Yep."

"You heard her say she loves me, didn't you?"

"Yep."

"Well, that ought to be worth more than me calling on her."

"Hah!" chortled Dusty. "Tryin' to welch on me, huh? Our bet was that you'd *court* her. Why, you ain't called at her house one time, son! You won't win the bet with kisses and *I love you's*." Dusty cackled again and abruptly left for his home.

When Matt London caught up with his deputy and began walking to the sheriff's office, Baker asked, "What did War Horse want, Matt?"

"He wanted to express his appreciation—and to tell me he and his braves would be back for the hangings."

Snow was beginning to fall from the leaden sky. As they moved along the street London said, "Will, I'm going to add a few more men to our guard tonight. And I'll keep them on duty until all three of the Van Horns have been hanged."

"I'll stay at the office tonight," volunteered Baker.

"No need," said London. "You've already been strained waiting for the Hatch gang to show up. You get yourself some rest tonight. There are enough men in this town to keep a dozen there at all times."

Entering the office, the two lawmen shook the snow off their coats and hats, and London went back to the cells.

Sam Van Horn was sitting on a bunk beside his ailing father, who was staring blankly into space. Baker had explained that he thought the elder Van Horn would need someone to care for him, and it might as well be his son. In the cell next to them Hale sat on his bunk, purple bruises on his face.

London walked over to Hale's cell. "I'm going to wire Helena for another judge. You'll have your trial as soon as he can get here."

Looking at the sheriff with hatred, Hale snarled, "Why bother with a trial? There were plenty of witnesses who saw me kill the judge. I'm goin' up against a stacked deck."

"The law says you get a trial," London answered flatly. "I intend to fulfill my duty and see that you do."

"Yeah," retorted Hale. "You're a big man when it comes to duty. You'll fulfill your duty hangin' my pa and my brother too, won't you? Don't it bother you to snuff out a man's life, Sheriff?"

"It isn't easy," replied London. "But this badge stands for the law, and that law has issued the sentences. As the man behind the badge, I will carry out the executions." He turned to go, then added, "Your father and Sam had their trial, and you'll have yours. That's more than they gave Yellow Bird . . . or than you gave Judge Southard."

When London left, Hale looked through the bars to the adjoining cell. "Don't you worry, Sam. Ben and Clete will find a way to get us out of here."

"I'm not so sure," contradicted Sam, touching his temples with shaky fingers. "There's no way Ben and Clete can cut through as many men as London has on guard. I'm afraid I'm gonna die in the mornin'."

"Don't despair, little brother," countered Hale. "Van Horns always come up with something."

Within an hour Matt London had a dozen men gathered at the sheriff's office, ready to stay until the hanging. Two men would be stationed outside the office at all times, though that post would be rotated frequently because of the cold. The sheriff warned them all to keep their eyes and ears peeled. Ben, Clete, and Jimmy Van Horn might try something at any time during the night.

After seeing the gallows pulled into place in the middle of the street, the two lawmen bid each other good night. Will Baker headed to his small house three blocks from the office, and Matt London moved briskly through the falling snow toward the warmth of his home, where Amy would welcome him with open arms.

As on other nights before a hanging, Amy would be especially attentive to him when he got home, trying to soothe him. He was always on edge when the time drew near for him to pull the trapdoor lever on the gallows. But it was his job as sheriff—and it was always at that moment that he felt the full weight of his badge.

Chapter Ten

Dawn came with a clear sky. Eight inches of fresh white snow were added to the old snow on the ground. The air was bitter cold, made worse by a merciless wind that ripped across the Montana plains, tormenting all who ventured out of doors with its icy talons.

Deputy Will Baker, refreshed after a good night's sleep, sat at his table drinking coffee while the light crept slowly through the frosted windows of the kitchen. He thought about what lay before him that morning. It was his job to walk the condemned man up the thirteen steps of the gallows, place the noose on his neck, and drop the black hood over his face. The job was distasteful, and Baker was glad Matt London was the one who had to trip the lever that actually plunged the victim to his death.

Baker got up and strapped on his six-gun. He pulled on his sheepskin coat, jammed his hat tight against his head, and slipped his hands into his gloves. Taking a deep breath, he stepped outside and closed the door.

A heavy club hissed through the cold air, connecting solidly with his head. Baker collapsed in a heap on the snow-covered porch.

The pale sun was lighting the frigid sky with fan-shaped rays as Matt London kissed his wife and trudged through the snow to the office. The dozen guards reported that all had been quiet through the night, but London told them to stay alert. He was glad to see that the men had a good fire going in the stove.

Dusty Canfield arrived, along with the Reverend Walter Elam, minister of the Billings Community Church. Dusty allowed Elam to enter first, and then the old-timer stepped in and closed the door behind him.

The minister got right to the point. "Sheriff, I have come to see Sam Van Horn before he goes to the gallows."

London nodded. "All right. Let's go back." He paused and looked back over his shoulder. "One of you men go out and clean the snow off the gallows steps. I don't want Sam to fall and break his neck."

No one knew whether to laugh or not.

As they approached Sam's cell the condemned man was pacing back and forth, icy sweat glistening on his brow in spite of the cold. "Reverend Elam is here to see you," London said quietly.

Sam swore vehemently. "I don't want to see no preacher! Get him out of here."

London looked at Elam and shrugged his shoulders. The minister nodded, and both men returned to the office, closing the door behind them.

After Elam had gone, Matt London eyed the clock on the wall. It was time to hang Sam Van Horn, and Will Baker had not shown up. It was not like his deputy to oversleep, but London figured that must be the case. He turned to one of the armed men. "Cal, run over to Will's house and see if he's about ready."

Cal Jenkins nodded and plunged out into the cold morning.

Stepping into the cellblock, the sheriff told Sam Van Horn that he had an extra few minutes to tell his father and brother good-bye. London then returned to the office.

Dusty Canfield cackled and tried to lighten the tension. "Wait'll I see ol' Will. Boy, am I gonna give him a hard time for oversleepin'!"

A few more minutes passed. Cal Jenkins came back, stomping snow from his boots. "Will must have already left, Sheriff. No one answered my knock, but from the footprints in the snow I could tell that he'd walked out the door."

London shook his head in wonderment. "Okay, let's go. We'll have to do it without him."

The waiting crowd watched as the dozen armed men filed out of the sheriff's office into the early morning sunlight, guns ready. At the same time Chief War Horse, Leaning Tree, and a few braves rode in and dismounted. Then Clete and Jimmy Van Horn rolled up in their wagon.

Inside the jail Matt London handcuffed Sam and led him from his cell. The young man was shaking with fear. "Dear God, help me! I don't want to die! I don't want to die!" he repeated over and over.

Hale's voice followed them. "Keep your chin up, Sam. The boys won't let us down."

With Hale's words resounding in his ears the sheriff threw Sam's coat over his shoulders and pushed him out the door. The cold air bit at their faces. Pausing among his men, London asked, "Seen anything?"

One man answered, "Clete and Jimmy are just sitting there in that wagon, Sheriff. We haven't seen Ben."

London looked up the street, hoping to see his deputy coming, but there was no sign of him. Again he cautioned his men to stay alert. Then throwing a glance at the two Van Horn brothers in the wagon, he nudged the condemned man, saying, "Okay, Sam. Let's go."

The crowd continued to swell as the sheriff prodded his frightened, whimpering prisoner up the steps of the gallows. Sam spotted his two brothers and was bewildered that they could sit there so casually. They had not even bothered to approach him before he mounted the stairs. But where was Ben? Sam sucked in a quivering breath when he saw the noose swaying in the wind above him. He froze on the eleventh step. From behind, London was shoving him onto the platform, positioning him on the trapdoor, when Sam noticed Holly standing beside her horse about thirty yards away, aloof from the crowd.

As London looped the stiff noose around his neck, Sam broke into sobs. Pulling the black hood from where he had tucked it under his belt, London said, "The Good Book says a man will reap what he sows, Sam. Too bad you had to learn that lesson the hard way."

Sam's sobs were muffled as the hood was dropped over his face and pulled tight with a drawstring. The crowd stood in silence against the cold as London descended the stairs. He moved to the lever, brushed the snow from it, and closed his gloved hand around it.

A distant voice cut the icy air. "Hold it, Sheriff!"

London looked up to see people scattering at the north end of the street. A hundred yards away, a wagon sat broadside in the middle of the street, and London was shocked to see that Will Baker was securely tied to it. Dynamite was attached to his upper body, held there with thin strands of twine. The separate fuses were wound into a central fuse barely two feet in length. Aghast, London stared at the scene, his hand frozen on the lever.

Defiantly puffing on a large cigar, Ben Van Horn stood beside the trussed-up deputy. His horse was a couple of steps away. "Hey, London!" shouted Ben. "Do you see what we have here?"

Like everyone else in the crowd—except Clete and Jimmy—Holly gasped, her hand going to her mouth.

"I've got your man here, London!" roared Ben. "In case your eyesight ain't too good, these here three little red sticks are *dynamite*—enough to blow your deputy into a million pieces. All I have to do is touch the tip of my cigar to this main fuse here, and in a few seconds . . . *boom!*" Holding the end of the fuse in one hand, he added, "There's just enough fuse to let me hop on my horse after I light it and get a safe distance away before the dynamite explodes. If you think you can run fast enough to put out the fuse, you better think again. Ain't no man that fast— especially through all this pretty new snow."

A chill ran up Holly's spine, and her heart started pounding. Dashing through the mesmerized crowd, she ran close to Matt London and shouted, "Ben! Don't be so foolish! You'll only make things worse!"

"Shut up, Holly!" retorted Ben, his breath vaporizing. "London, are you listenin' to me?"

"I'm listening," called the sheriff, anger and fear clawing at him.

"Release Sam right now."

Through the black hood over Sam's head came the sound of his laughter. "Come on, Sheriff!" he cried with elation. "Get me off of here!"

"Let Sam get my pa and Hale," continued Ben, holding the burning cigar in his free hand, "then Clete and Jimmy will put 'em in the wagon and drive away. Once they're out of town, I'll follow 'em and leave Baker unharmed. But I warn you—if it doesn't happen right now, and to the letter, I'll blow Baker to kingdom come!"

London's hand was still on the lever that controlled the trapdoor. He squinted, studying the fuse Ben was holding, gauging its length.

Dusty saw that the sheriff was weighing the situation in his mind. Limping up beside him, the old-timer whispered hoarsely, "Matthew, you're not thinkin' what I'm thinkin' you're thinkin', are you?"

The lanky, rawboned sheriff spoke through lips that hardly moved, not taking his eyes from the scene up the street. "I've always been a pretty fast runner, Dusty."

"But Matthew," whined the old man, "Ben's right. It's too far. That there fuse is mighty short, and you gotta plow through all that snow too."

Sam's muffled voice penetrated the air again, demanding that he be released. Apart from that and the murmur of London's and Dusty's voices, a horrified hush had fallen over the crowd.

Matt London's dark eyes were fierce as he rasped to Dusty, "I've never let an outlaw intimidate me. I'm not about to start now."

"But Matthew," argued Dusty, "Will's life is at stake. Don't let your dadburned pride—"

The old man's words were cut short as London shouted to Ben, "If you light that fuse, mister, I'll hunt you down like a mangy cur! You'll hang too! Now, back off!"

"I ain't backin' off," yelled Van Horn. "Do as I tell you this instant, or I'm lightin' the fuse."

Will Baker, straining against the ropes that held him, finally spoke up. "Matt!" he shouted. "Don't back down! We can't give in to jackals like this!"

Ben looked at the deputy and then called, "Sheriff, you've got ten seconds to let Sam go!"

"Ben!" Holly's voice carried along the street again. "If you light that fuse, you are nothing less than a cold-blooded murderer."

Ben's lips went tight. "Which side are you on anyway, Holly? That's your flesh and blood up there with a rope around his neck."

Shouting back at her brother, Holly said, "I'm on the side of the law, where you ought to be, Ben."

"Well, in that case you're no longer my sister," he roared. "You're a dirty traitor!"

He looked at the deputy for a moment, and the two appeared to be exchanging words. Then, looking back down the street, he shouted, "Hey, you know what, London? If you don't let Sam go, *you* are gonna kill your man here!"

Dusty Canfield could see what was coming. Matt London felt he could run the hundred yards in time to put out the fuse.

The sheriff knew it was a gamble, of course, but he also knew that to give in to Ben Van Horn's demands would open the door for other outlaws to try the same thing. He did not dare to allow the belligerent Dutchman to intimidate him. *Besides, even Will has told me not to back down,* he thought.

The sheriff readied himself. Knowing that the enraged outlaw would immediately light the fuse, London shouted, "No deal!" and while the words were coming from his mouth, he pulled the lever and dashed toward his deputy. As Sam's body plummeted the crowd gasped.

Ben swore and touched the hot tip of the cigar to the fuse. It crackled and flared into a tiny, hissing ball of fire. Still swearing, Ben bolted to his horse, leaped in the saddle, and galloped away.

Holly gave a weak cry and without forethought started through the snow toward Baker.

"Miss Holly!" Dusty Canfield yelled. "Stay back!"

Matt London's heart felt as if it were being squeezed by a cold hand as he ran, and the frigid air he was sucking in seemed to tear his lungs apart. Suddenly his feet slipped on the snow and flew out from under him. He rolled twice, losing his hat, and was up running again, wishing he had time to remove his heavy coat.

Meanwhile Holly, hypnotized by the scene in front of her, paid no attention to Dusty's plea but kept on moving forward, faltering through the snow.

Baker, aware that his boss and Holly were both racing toward him, broke into an icy sweat in spite of the subzero air. He knew that London had to reach him before the central fuse burned up. Once it got beyond that point, it would spread in three different directions. There would never be time to snuff out all the fuses. Both he and the sheriff would die. He did not want Holly caught in the blast as well.

Shifting his eyes between the flame and Matt London, Will Baker felt a strange distortion of time. London seemed to move in a thick, exaggerated motion, as if time had slowed, while the flame seemed to be moving in a realm in which time had speeded up.

He began to doubt that his boss could make it. The flame was crawling along too fast. Lifting his voice, he shouted, "Matt! You can't make it! Hit the ground and take cover!"

But Matt London, determined to save his deputy's life, barreled forward, throwing all the strength he could muster into his legs.

The flame was almost at the joint. Again Will Baker cried out, "Matt! Stop! Get back, you can't make it!"

Holly kept slowly moving toward them, watching with her heart in her mouth, listening to the deputy screaming for London to stop and hit the ground. Behind her the crowd stood in absolute silence.

Suddenly Holly's breath seemed to catch in her throat. As London drew near Baker his body blocked her view of the smoking fuse. She could not bear to watch. Halting in her tracks, she covered her eyes with her hands and waited for the explosion.

With his lungs on fire and his legs beginning to feel as though they were full of lead, Matt London reached Baker—just as the flame touched the ends of the individual fuses. In desperation he snuffed the flame by gripping it in his gloved hand.

The crowd waited, knowing if there was going to be an explosion, it would happen within two or three seconds. Clete and Jimmy craned their necks to see what was happening.

Holly realized the explosion should have come by now. She parted her fingers fearfully and looked through them. She saw London tearing away the fuses and Will Baker sagging against the ropes that bound him to the wagon.

"Will!" she shouted, bounding forward. Her cry was mingled with the cheers of the crowd behind her.

The townspeople followed Holly in running toward Matt London, who was puffing and untying his sweating deputy. At the rear of the crowd Dusty Canfield hobbled painfully on his bad leg.

Panting, Holly reached the lawmen first, just as the rope fell off Will Baker. She plunged into his arms, weeping. They held each other tight while she sobbed over and over that she loved him.

Will Baker ran his dry tongue over his even drier lips and gasped, "Matt, that . . . that was a close one."

Relief was evident in the sheriff's voice as he said between ragged breaths, "Yeah. Close."

Baker was unable to work up any saliva in his mouth. With dry tongue he said, "Ben clubbed me from behind . . . when I came out my door."

"And I thought you had overslept," London wheezed, angry with himself for not knowing better.

Holly smothered Baker with kisses. "Oh, darling," she gasped. "I was so afraid Matt wouldn't make it. I love you! I don't ever want to lose you."

Baker found that he was able to laugh a little. "Lose me, honey? Just *try* to get rid of me!"

While London caught his breath, fury toward Ben Van Horn began to boil up within him. That vile excuse for a human being was going to pay for this sadistic deed. But mixed with his wrath was satisfaction that Sam Van Horn had been punished for his crime in spite of Ben's effort to free him. London was also pleased that the other two Van Horns remained in his jail.

Looking back down the street, the sheriff called to his armed guards, some of whom remained near the gallows, "Hey, men! Take Clete and Jimmy Van Horn into custody."

"They're not here, Sheriff," one of them called back. "They took off the instant you put out the fuse."

London nodded and waved that he understood. He turned to Baker and Holly, who were still embracing. "Holly, after what Ben said to you, I'm not sure of what he might do. It won't be safe for you to be at your farm. Besides, I've got to take a posse there and go after all three of them. I'd rather you wouldn't be there when I do."

"You're probably right, Sheriff," she said with a weak smile, "but I have nowhere else to go."

"If you don't mind sharing a bedroom with Sandra, you can move into our house."

Thinking about the offer for a few seconds, Holly said, "I appreciate your kindness, Sheriff. I'll make other arrangements as soon as possible."

Matt London was reading Will Baker's eyes. Though the deputy stood quietly, the sheriff could plainly see what he was thinking. Baker would give the situation a little more time, and then he would offer Holly a permanent home—as Mrs. William Baker.

By now the townspeople were all gathered about London, congratulating their sheriff on his tremendous feat.

Dusty Canfield, sucking hard for air, finally reached his friend. Moving close to Baker and Holly, he said with a twinkle in his eye, "It's a dadburned good thing Matthew can run so fast, Deputy. Because if you'd been outta the picture, I'd have courted this gorgeous little lady myself!"

There was a round of laughter as the group moved through the crowd. Baker ushered Holly to her horse and helped her into the saddle as London said to her, "Ride over to my house and tell Amy what happened. Tell her you need a place to stay for a while. She'll be glad to have you. Oh, and tell her I'll be home shortly."

Holly rode away, avoiding a look at the gallows, where Sam's body was still hanging.

When London, Baker, and Dusty reached the office, the army of men was still maintaining their vigil both inside and outside. London asked the two who were outside to help the undertaker remove Sam's body. The rest of them were to continue to stand guard until the other three Van Horns were behind bars—or until Hale and Barth Van Horn were both hanged. London then expressed his appreciation to the men and went back to the cellblock.

From the bunks in their cells Barth and Hale Van Horn looked at the sheriff with hatred in their eyes. "Anybody come back here to let you know what happened out there?" London asked them.

Hale stood up and walked to the bars. "No," he grunted, "but I know by the look in your eyes it ain't good."

"That sort of depends on your point of view," London told them.

The two men listened in silence as the sheriff gave them a brief rundown of Ben's attempt to free them, ending with, "But you men are still in here, and Sam has gone to meet his maker."

Van Horn groaned in torment, while Hale swore under his breath, swinging a thick fist through the air.

London was unsympathetic. As he ran his angry gaze between the two Van Horns, his voice was biting. "We're going to bring in the others. Ben is going to stand trial for attempted murder, and Clete and Jimmy will face charges as accessories. Hear me, and hear me good. *Nobody* walks out of my jail without first paying his dues!"

Chapter Eleven

Sheriff Matt London left the cellblock and returned to his office, where his men were waiting. To his deputy he said, "Will, pick five or six men to go with us as a posse. The others will be enough to guard the prisoners."

Leaving Will Baker to his task, the sheriff walked home to find Holly Van Horn already settled in. Amy was glad to have her, and Sandra was delighted with her temporary roommate. London told the women that he was taking a posse after the Van Horn brothers, and he expressed his sorrow to Holly and Sandra that things had turned out so badly for them.

London and Amy went into their room to spend a few minutes alone. Holding her husband in her arms and kissing him tenderly, Amy told him to be careful; the Van Horns had turned into savage killers with nothing left to lose, she said. He assured her that he would use extreme caution.

Twenty minutes later the sheriff, his deputy, and six possemen rode out of Billings toward the Van Horn farm. Arriving at the place, they found it deserted, with cold ashes in the stoves. The Van Horn brothers, knowing London would be after them, had apparently gone into hiding, though the sheriff doubted that they had gone very far since Barth and Hale Van Horn were still incarcerated in Billings.

After every building had been searched, Will Baker

said, "Matt, I think we need to start checking out the surrounding farms and ranches. They have to be somewhere near."

"My thinking exactly," the sheriff said. "Let's start at the Bryant place."

George and Alice Bryant invited the lawmen and their posse into the farmhouse to warm themselves around the huge potbellied stove in the parlor. While Alice served coffee, London told them what had happened in town and explained that the three Van Horn brothers were on the dodge. Since the brothers were not at the Van Horn place, the lawmen were checking all the nearby farms and ranches.

When London had finished explaining their mission, the Bryants shook their heads and told him that they had not seen the Van Horns.

Braving the bitter cold and the biting wind, the eight men rode off, stopping at the farms of Mort Peabody, Albert Winter, and Jake Nye. Nobody had seen anything of the Van Horn brothers.

As the posse rode back toward town the sky was thick with gray clouds, and the feel of snow was in the air. Another storm was brewing.

London called for a meeting of the townsmen when he got back to Billings. He had no doubt that the Van Horn brothers were planning to break their father and brother out of the jail, he explained to the townsmen, so they all had to continue their guard vigil around the clock, working in shifts of eight.

In addition, London explained that he still needed another half dozen men to ride with Will Baker and himself as they continued searching for the Van Horns. There were more than enough volunteers.

The next morning a storm hit the Montana plains in full fury, preventing the sheriff and his men from setting out on their search. Waiting out the storm, Matt London paced the floor of his office, frustrated by the delay. Two days later, with another fifteen inches of new snow on the ground, the posse set out. For the next three days they covered most of the county, even checking again with the first four farmers. But their search was fruitless; it was as if the Van Horn brothers had vanished into thin air.

On the day before Barth Van Horn was to hang, the posse rode back into town with red noses and blue lips just as the sun was setting on the western horizon. While the others headed for home, the two lawmen went to the sheriff's office.

Dusty Canfield was among the guards. The old man was just spitting into the cuspidor when London and Baker came in with a blast of cold air. "No luck, Matthew?" he asked.

Shaking his head, the sheriff said, "It's crazy. Nobody has seen those three, but I know as sure as I'm standing here that they're somewhere in the area. They know Barth is being hanged in the morning, and they're not going to let it happen without trying to prevent it."

"Matthew, it looks like we're just gonna have to let 'em come to us."

"You're right, Dusty," London said, nodding. "They're going to pull something dirty when they come too." Rubbing his chin, he said, "I've been thinking. Those three might go after Holly and Sandra—even try to involve them in the breakout. Dusty, I need a man who can handle a shotgun to stay at my house with the women after I leave for the hanging in the morning."

The old man's wrinkled face lit up. Eyes sparkling, he limped to where his shotgun leaned against the wall, picked it up, and said, "You mean a man with a shotgun like Fanny May here?"

"Are you volunteering?"

"You're dadblamed tootin' I am!" exclaimed Dusty, shifting his plug from one side of his mouth to the other. Scratching the gray stubble on his chin, he said, "You can bank on it, Matthew. Them women will be absolutely safe with me and Fanny May around."

London chuckled. "Yeah, but will *you* be safe with

those three women? As handsome and irresistible as you
are, they just might attack you." Through their laughter
London added, "On second thought, maybe I better get a
man who isn't so attractive."

Dusty ran a sleeve across his mouth. "You won't, though,"
he cackled. "Because you know I can handle a shotgun
better than any man in this town. I'll be there at dawn."

Matt and Amy London sat on an ornate, overstuffed
couch in front of their fireplace. Holly and Sandra had
tactfully gone to bed, leaving the sheriff and his wife
alone. Amy looked at her husband, the firelight dancing
on his angular face, accentuating the hollows in his rugged
cheeks. "Matt," she said softly.

"Hmm?" he said, holding his gaze on the fire.

"When things like this Van Horn situation happen, do
you wish you'd chosen another profession?"

Facing his wife, London watched the flickering light
play on Amy's long black hair. "What do you mean?"
he asked.

"I mean . . . as brutal as those men are—wrapping your
deputy in dynamite and that kind of thing—does it sometimes make you wish you didn't wear a badge?"

"I won't say the thought doesn't cross my mind when
things get tough," he said. "But . . . no. I've never really
wished I hadn't pinned on a badge." Studying her shining
eyes for a moment, he asked, "Do *you* wish I weren't a
lawman?"

Amy ran her fingers through his thick, curly hair. Twirl-
ing a heavy lock around her fingers, she said, "I won't tell
you that being a lawman's wife is a Sunday picnic—it's
pretty frightening in fact. Every time you walk out that
door, I have to crowd dark thoughts from my mind about
never seeing you again. To be honest, I am terrified to
think what the Van Horn brothers might do tomorrow to
spring their father and brother. I wish it were all over.
But to answer your question . . . no. I don't wish you
weren't a lawman. You wear that badge because it's your

chosen profession. Not only that, you are the very best
there is. I am proud of what you are, and I love you with
all my heart. As long as you wear that badge, I will *want*
you to wear it."

Grinning broadly, Matt London cuffed his wife's cheek
playfully. Then pulling her to him, he breathed, "I love
you, Mrs. London. No man ever had a wife as wonderful
as you." His heart throbbed as he felt Amy's warm breath
on his mouth. For a few moments their tender and pas-
sionate kiss carried them to another world . . . a world
without guns, jails, killings, gallows, or Van Horns.

There was merely a hint of dawn as Sheriff Matt London
sat at his kitchen table drinking coffee. The smell of bacon
frying filled the room as the three women moved about
the kitchen, each doing her part to prepare breakfast.
Holly was dressed in one of Amy's robes, a light blue one.
London's heart went out to the lovely blonde, carrying the
weight of knowing that her father was going to hang in a
little more than an hour. As mean and brutal as Barth Van
Horn was, he was Holly's father, and she had to be hurting inside—though she apparently was trying hard not to
show it.

And then there was poor Sandra, hated by her husband
and made to feel an outcast. Sandra wore Amy's old faded
yellow robe. It made her long black hair look even blacker.

London's eyes lighted on the woman he loved. Amy was
clad in her new bright red robe—the one he liked best.
The brilliant color highlighted her soft, creamy skin—and
the way it fit accentuated her small waist.

While the sheriff was draining his coffee cup there was a
loud knock at the door. He stood up and headed toward it,
whipping out his revolver as a precaution. "That's probably Dusty," he said to the women, who had stopped what
they were doing.

The old man stepped in, cursing the cold and stomping
snow from his boots. He walked into the kitchen and
leaned Fanny May against the wall. When he peeled off

his coat and hung it over a chair, London noticed that the coat pockets were bulging with shotgun shells.

Laughing, the sheriff said, "You planning to fight a war, are you?"

"I come prepared," Dusty replied flatly, and then he sniffed loudly. Tossing his dirty old hat on top of his coat, he moved to the stove, the source of the aroma that was tempting his nostrils. "Good mornin', ladies," he cackled. "I'll be able to protect you better if'n I do it on a full stomach."

The old-timer's presence seemed to lift everybody's spirits. Just as Dusty sat down at the table there was another knock at the door. Again London drew his revolver, and Dusty stood up and grabbed his shotgun. As the sheriff moved cautiously toward the door, the old man hobbled behind him.

Gun ready, London called out, "Who is it?"

"It's only me," came a familiar voice.

The door came open, revealing the tall, lanky form of Deputy Will Baker. He headed toward Holly while greeting the others. Folding her into his arms, he said, "I just had to come by and tell you I'm sorry for what has to happen this morning . . . and to tell you that I love you."

"Holly," London put in softly, "I, too, am truly sorry about what I have to do today. I wish someone else could pull the lever, but it's my job."

Holly touched the sheriff's arm. Looking into his eyes, she said, "You are only doing your duty. I love my father, but he brought this on himself." She sighed. "I'd like to see him, but I don't think I could bear it. And I'd only be scorned as a traitor to the family."

Holly and Will Baker went into the living room to have a few moments alone together, while London gave instructions to Dusty Canfield. The doors were to be bolted, the sheriff ordered, and were not to be opened unless Dusty knew who was outside. If there was any trouble, he should not hesitate to shoot; the women must be protected at all costs.

When his deputy and Holly returned to the kitchen, London provided the blond woman with one of his Colt .45's, knowing she was adept with handguns.

Will Baker kissed Holly, and then he walked outside, looking up at the thick, leaden sky that was spitting snow.

The sheriff, now in his heavy coat and wearing hat, scarf, and gloves, stepped out on the porch with his wife, the brutally cold air assaulting them. They kissed and embraced momentarily, then London said, "Get in the house, honey. It's much too cold out here."

Amy pulled him to her and kissed him again. "Be careful."

"Don't worry, I will," the sheriff replied and stepped off the porch.

The two lawmen trudged through the snow toward their office. When they reached the corner, London looked back. Despite the well-below-zero temperature, Amy was still on the porch, looking like a Christmas doll in her bright red robe, a breeze tugging at her long dark hair. She waved and called, "I love you, Matt! I love you!"

London waved back, then he and his deputy turned the corner.

As they moved through the falling snow Baker said, "You two are really devoted, aren't you?"

"That beautiful woman is the most important thing in my life. I would do anything for her. I mean anything."

"I hope Holly and I will have a love like that, Matt."

"Let me tell you something, my boy. Marriage will intensify your love a million times over. By the way, *have* you two talked matrimony?"

"Not yet," replied Baker. "But I'm going to speak to Holly after all this hanging is done and her time of grieving is over."

Thirty minutes later, with snow still falling lightly and daylight filtering through a gunmetal-gray sky, Barth Van Horn was led from the sheriff's office, surrounded by a phalanx of well-armed men. From inside the cellblock Hale's muffled voice could be heard as he called, "Hang on, Pa! The boys won't let you down!"

The twenty-below temperature held the spectators to a minimum. Not more than thirty people had turned out. Sheriff Matt London kept searching up and down the street, remembering all too clearly what had happened one week before, but there was no activity at either end of the street.

The sheriff's attention was drawn to a single Crow Indian, one of the lesser chiefs of the tribe, who came riding in on his pinto. London decided that War Horse must have sent Lone Bear as his representative to witness the hanging.

As Will Baker ushered a weak-kneed Barth Van Horn up the thirteen steps of the gallows amid lightly falling snow, Lone Bear dismounted and moved toward the sheriff. London smiled, and the Indian nodded impassively. Speaking in the flat gutturals of the Crow, Lone Bear said, "Chief War Horse sent Lone Bear to watch execution, Matt London. Lone Bear is to tell you of War Horse's appreciation. Yellow Bird's murderers have paid for their crime as you promised."

"I will always keep my word to your chief," London said, smiling.

Lone Bear walked away and stood by himself to observe the hanging.

While the sheriff was talking with the Indian, Will Baker was preparing to drop the noose over Barth Van Horn's head. No one was paying attention to the north end of town. Just as the sheriff turned toward the lever that controlled the trapdoor of the gallows, a horse carrying Jimmy Van Horn came galloping down the street. Trailing two riderless horses on a rope, the youngest Van Horn shouted, "Sheriff! Sheriff! Before your deputy puts the noose on Pa's neck, you'd better look up the street!"

Matt London was not going to give the Van Horn brothers a chance to get an edge on him. Before looking, London called, "Will, get that noose over his head!"

London gripped the lever, then swung his gaze north. A wagon was standing broadside, as before, but this time it was another hundred yards farther away, just beyond the town. He squinted through the floating snowflakes and then widened his eyes. Terror etched itself on his face, while his blood turned to ice.

"*Amy!*" he gasped.

Though the distance was too great to make her out clearly, Matt London recognized the bright red robe and the long black hair that fell over her shoulders. Just as Will Baker had been wrapped in dynamite during the Van Horn's last attempt, Amy was wrapped in it now and tied to the wagon. Ben and Clete Van Horn stood beside the wagon defiantly, both of them smoking cigars.

Jimmy Van Horn walked his horse to where the sheriff stood and looked down at the lawman with wicked eyes. His deliberate words were as foreboding as a death knell: "The fuse is even shorter than before, but my brothers will still have time to get away after it is lit. If you try to outrun the fuse this time, your wife will die. It's too far, London. You'll never make it."

Matt London felt as though he were trapped in some horrible nightmare. This could not be happening. It could not be real.

A gust of icy wind slapped the face of the stunned man with cold contempt, clearing his senses. It was all real. Amy was in the hands of the vile Van Horns! The sheriff swallowed hard. He cursed himself for leaving just one old man with the women.

Up on the gallows Will Baker stood beside Barth Van Horn, who, despite the rope around his neck, had a sly smile curving his mouth. The deputy's unbelieving eyes assessed the scene at the edge of town. The Van Horn brothers had stooped to an all-time low. Will Baker wondered what they had done with Dusty Canfield—and if Sandra and Holly were all right.

Jimmy Van Horn's cold voice spoke again. "You are going to release my pa and Hale, Sheriff. Now! If you don't, Ben and Clete will touch off the dynamite."

A wave of nausea washed over Matt London. Amy's

black hair blowing in the wind reminded him of her standing on the porch a little more than thirty minutes before in that same robe, waving and calling that she loved him. She had to be freezing with little more than the robe to cover her body. A silent, primal scream tore through the depths of his being. Demonic hatred burst forth in his breast toward the Van Horn brothers . . . a hatred such as Matthew London had never felt in his thirty-three years.

The youthful Van Horn continued, "Ben wants me to tell you that when Pa and Hale and I reach the wagon where your wife is, we will ride out slowly. You are to wait five minutes before you go to her. If you or anyone else moves in her direction before those five minutes are up, we will shoot your wife in the back. There's dynamite tied behind her too."

Matt London's eyes glinted, contrasting with the ashen gray of his skin. He wanted to crush the smart-mouthed kid on the horse and his two brothers standing insolently beside Amy two hundred yards away.

"Now tell your deputy to take the rope off Pa's neck, Sheriff," Jimmy went on. "Let him come down and climb on one of these horses. While he's doing that, I want Hale brought out here. Try any tricks, lawman, and you'll need a magnifying glass to pick up your wife's pieces!"

London was numb all over as he recalled how Ben Van Horn had lit the fuse on Baker. The man would not hesitate to do it again; killing Amy would not penetrate his savage conscience. London knew Jimmy was right. There was no way he could cover two hundred yards and snuff out the fuse. He had barely made it the last time at half the distance.

The small crowd, including Lone Bear, fixed their eyes on Matt London. The sheriff glanced at the impassive face of the Indian. The words he had just spoken to him echoed through his head: *I will always keep my word to your chief.* If London succumbed to the Van Horns' demands, his promise to War Horse would be broken. He would also be going back on the oath he took when he pinned on the badge. He would not be upholding the law to the best of his ability.

The sheriff looked at the townspeople who had entrusted him with their safety. And the armed men who had risked their own lives to stand by him waited now to see what he would do.

His eyes found Will Baker standing on the gallows platform next to Barth Van Horn, outlined against the dismal gray sky. When it had been Baker wrapped in dynamite, London had pulled the lever.

But this time it was different! It was *Amy* whose life was threatened. The sheriff weighed the desperate situation in his mind. If he gave in and released the killers, he would no longer deserve to wear the badge that was pinned to his chest. His deputy would be disappointed in him. The townspeople would look down on him, and War Horse would be angry. His career as a lawman would be over.

Matt London made his decision. Little more than a half hour ago he had said as much to Baker. *That beautiful woman is the most important thing in my life. I would do anything for her. I mean anything.*

London looked past Jimmy Van Horn to the wagon two hundred yards away. His love for Amy was too strong. She meant more to him than his reputation, his honor—even his life.

He had to give the command while he still wore the badge. Looking up at his deputy, he said, "Turn Barth loose, Will. Then go inside and let Hale out."

Will Baker immediately removed the noose from Van Horn's neck and took the handcuffs from his wrists. Jimmy grinned triumphantly. No one in the crowd said a word. Lone Bear's face was still an impassive mask.

The deputy hurried down the steps of the gallows and ran into the jail. The crowd remained mute as big Barth Van Horn lumbered down the steps slowly and headed for one of the horses Jimmy had brought. Settling into the saddle, he gave the sheriff a wicked smile.

In those few short moments Matt London thought about

his future. He would have to leave Montana and find another way to make a living. He and Amy would have to go someplace where no one knew them and start over. But it would be all right, he told himself. He and Amy would be together; he could take anything as long as they were together.

Hale Van Horn emerged from the jail with a sneer of triumph on his face. Mounting the horse, he looked hatefully at London. "I've been waitin' for this moment. You're gonna be sorry you ever laid eyes on me, tin star." Then emitting a devilish laugh, he said, "What was that you said, London? Nobody walks out of your jail without payin' his dues?"

Hale was still laughing fiendishly as he followed his father and Jimmy northward through town. Feeling the eyes of the crowd and Lone Bear on him, the sheriff ignored the escaping prisoners. He intently watched the scene at the wagon. He noticed that Ben's and Clete's horses were standing nearby to carry them away. A burning thought welled up: *There won't be a safe place in this world for you Van Horns. Sometime, someplace the law will catch up with you.*

Matt London yearned to run to his wife. She had to be freezing by now. She was too far away for him to see the fear on her face, but he knew it was there.

The Van Horns seemed to move so slowly. "Hurry up!" he half whispered. "Get out of here! I want to go to Amy!"

Barth, Hale, and Jimmy finally reached the wagon, and Ben and Clete mounted up, puffing on their cigars. London's eyes were glued to the scene. Hale seemed to be talking to Ben and Clete, but then suddenly, with quick, determined moves, he slipped from his saddle and grabbed Ben's cigar. He turned in the sheriff's direction for a moment and then walked to Amy—and touched the smoking tip of the cigar to the fuse.

As smoke began to issue from the hissing flame Amy twisted against the rope that held her fast, and she screamed. Nearby, Hale leaped into his saddle, and the gang galloped away.

Matt London's eyes bulged in stark horror. With an icy hand squeezing his spine he bolted toward the wagon, crying, *"Amy-y-y-y!"*

Every fiber in his body was strained as London raced toward his wife, his heart pounding like a runaway triphammer as he screamed her name. Watching the black smoke billowing upward from the fuse, he ran. His legs ached, begging for relief, and his lungs seemed to have caught fire, but he ran. For the love of Amy—for the *life* of Amy—he ran.

Will Baker entered the race, but he was charging after his boss, trying to stop him. There was no possible way London could reach his wife—and if he was too close when the dynamite blew, London would also be killed.

London barreled forward, unaware that his deputy was coming behind him. The crowd looked on, transfixed. Amy kept twisting her head and screaming, her long black hair hanging over her face.

The sheriff sprinted past the spot where the wagon had stood a week before. The flame had eaten up the two-foot central fuse and was igniting the individual fuses.

London became vaguely aware of Will Baker's voice behind him, shouting for him to stop, warning that he could not make it. But on he ran, his eyes riveted to the woman in the bright red robe with the long black hair covering her face. His legs were weakening. *Can't stop!* he told himself. *Can't stop!* He could feel the pounding of his pulse. Calling on reserves deep within him, he ran even faster.

The helpless young woman was coughing and screaming as the smoke enveloped her head. Sparking flames were crawling up all the fuses, spreading in every direction. They were closing in fast on the deadly dynamite.

Pressing on with every ounce of his strength, London focused on the hissing fuses and ran. He was within fifty yards when the flames were about to reach the half-dozen sticks of dynamite. Staring at the burning fuses, he wailed, *"Amy-y-y-y! No-o-o! Amy-y-y-y!"* There was a moment's ominous hush, and then thunder split his mind as the dynamite exploded in a series of rapid, booming concussions. The impact knocked him to the ground, with Will Baker going down ten yards behind him.

Struggling to pull his senses together, London heard Baker calling his name above the ringing in his ears, but the deputy's voice seemed to come from miles away. Lifting his head, London watched pieces of debris falling earthward. Among them, little bits of red robe were scattered about.

In a state of shock London scrambled to his feet and started toward what was left of his wife. Suddenly strong hands seized him, and he heard the familiar voice of his deputy, saying, "No, Matt! Don't look. Come on, let's go back."

The sheriff's mind was totally muddled. He wrestled Baker for a moment, but then he quit struggling and gave in. Stumbling and groping, he let himself be pushed toward town. His eyes were fixed in a vacant stare, seeing nothing.

Chapter Twelve

T he exploding dynamite rapidly drew the sequestered citizens of Billings from their trembling houses. From every direction they ran toward the center of town to the small, horrified group gathered near the gallows, who gave them the sad news of Amy London's brutal murder. With their fingers pointing up the street as they talked, the growing crowd watched Will Baker guide Matt London toward them, away from the devastation.

The crowd, speaking words of solace and comfort to the sheriff, parted for him and his deputy as they drew near. But Matt London was unable to comprehend their words.

Dr. John Alton, who was present in his official capacity as coroner because of the scheduled hanging, took charge. Alton took one look into the sheriff's eyes and knew the man was in deep shock. "Let's get him to my office," he said quickly to Baker.

"I'd rather take him home, Doc," said the deputy. "I'm hoping Holly and Sandra are there and can take care of him." He shook his head, worried. "We left Dusty there to guard the women, but since the Van Horns got Amy, I'm not sure what we'll find."

"Well, let's get over there and find out," the doctor said, taking hold of London's arm.

Art Anderson, chairman of Billings's town council, came over to them and said, "Will, I'll form a posse so we can go after the Van Horns."

"Good," responded Baker. "I'll join you as soon as I get Matt home."

Across the street Lone Bear silently looked upon the scene from beside his pinto. Seeing that it would be of no use to try to talk with the sheriff, he mounted and rode away.

When Baker and Alton helped the sheriff onto the porch of his house, they noticed immediately that the door was ajar. Leaving the doctor to guide London inside, Baker darted through each room, swinging upstairs and down. But no one was there, and the house was cold.

Rugs were crumpled. Tables and chairs were overturned. A kerosene lamp was shattered on the floor, its fuel having soaked into a braided rug. Dr. Alton sat London down on the overstuffed couch just as Baker returned. "Doc, there's nobody here. They've—"

Suddenly there was a thumping noise, coming from a large hall closet. The deputy ran to it and flung open the door.

Dusty Canfield was tied up and gagged. There was a gash on his forehead, surrounded by a large purple lump. His eyes were wild, and he was making a whining noise through the gag.

Baker pulled off the gag first and then began untying him. "How did this happen, Dusty?"

Swearing vehemently, the old man said, "Them dirty dudes tricked me, Will! They must've been hidin', watchin' you and Matthew walk away. They made me think it was you and him come back. When I opened the door, they come in like a herd of buffalo and slammed me in the head. Where are the women?"

"I was hoping you could tell me. Looks like they took Holly and Sandra with them."

"What about Amy?"

Baker swallowed hard. "She's dead."

"Dead?"

As he helped the old man over to the couch, the deputy told him what had happened. Dusty swore and began to weep. Sitting him down next to London, Baker said to Alton, "Doc, I've got to lead the posse. Do you want me to send someone to help you care for these two?"

Alton shook his head. "I don't think so. Dusty's tough. He'll be all right. If I need anything, he can handle it. I'll stay with Matt until the shock wears off and he's back to himself."

The clamor of horses' hooves indicated the posse had come. One of the men had Baker's horse in tow. As the deputy swung into his saddle he told his men that the Van Horns had taken Holly and Sandra with them. Talking above their angry comments, Baker reminded them that the entire area had already been combed in search of the Van Horns' hiding place. They would try to follow the trail and then go to the Van Horn place, but if the outlaws were not found almost immediately, the fast-falling snow would quickly obliterate all trace of them.

Art Anderson spoke up. "We couldn't stay out for too long in this cold anyway without packing a lot of provisions. If we aren't back by sundown, I don't know who'd freeze to death sooner—me or my horse."

Will Baker set his jaw and tightened his hat on his head. Speaking with a rasp in his voice, he said, "Sooner or later I'm going to find them. Nothing is going to stop me. And nobody is going to keep Holly from me. I'm going to get her back."

The next morning, after three more inches of snow had fallen during the night, the sun rose into a cold, crystal-clear sky. The temperature was twenty-two degrees below zero.

Matt London stared at the gleaming oak coffin while the Reverend Walter Elam read from the Bible. The undertaker had placed what had remained of Amy's body in the coffin and sealed it up.

Despite the cold, most of the townspeople and neighboring farmers and ranchers had turned out for the funeral in the town cemetery. Dusty Canfield and Will Baker

flanked the sheriff, and Dr. John Alton stood behind him.
The doctor had stayed with London the day before until
the sheriff responded and could talk normally. Dusty had
stayed with his friend when the doctor left, and he was
joined by Will Baker when the posse had returned from
another futile search for the Van Horns. Dusty and Baker
had remained at the London home all night.

When the ceremony was over, the townspeople came
up to Matt London to express their sympathy for his tragic
loss. The many kind words spoken about Amy were too
much for London to bear, and he wept openly.

When the last person had passed by, London turned to
his deputy and said, "I'm going to the office. Will you get
Art and bring him there?"

"Sure." Baker nodded. "Right away." He clamped a
hand on Dusty's shoulder as the old man limped alongside
the sheriff, fiddling with the bandage on his head.

As he and Dusty walked, London was deep in thought.
He kept reliving the terrible event: Amy's screaming as
the flame crawled up the fuses . . . the sickening sound of
the rapid explosions and the instant fire and smoke . . .
the deathly silence that followed.

Shaking his head to dislodge the picture, London gave
in to the hatred that was boiling like a volcano within him.
The cords of his neck were taut and swollen, and he felt as
though his insides were on fire. The Van Horns were
going to pay. This world was not a big enough place for
them to hide. He would find them, and they would rue
the day they were born. *Especially Hale*, he thought. Hale
would die an inch at a time.

By the time he and Dusty reached the sheriff's office,
Matt London's teeth were hurting, he had been clenching
them so hard. Dusty remarked that the fire in the stove
was about out, and he went to restore it. Seconds later
Baker and Anderson came in.

"You wanted to see me, Matt?" queried Anderson.

Peeling off his sheepskin coat and dropping his hat on
the desk, London said, "Yeah, Art. I'm turning in my
badge."

Anderson's jaw sagged. Dusty dropped a log on his foot and swore. Will Baker stood owl-eyed, wondering if he had heard correctly.

"You'll have to set up a county election, Art," London proceeded. "Select a new sheriff. Will can handle the job until you do. In fact, I recommend you run Will for sheriff. He's the best."

Dusty screwed up his face and squeaked, "Matthew, you're talkin' like a madman! What do you mean, you're turnin' in your badge?"

"Just what I said," came the flat reply.

"But *why*?" demanded Baker, visibly upset.

"That's what *I* would like to know," chimed in Anderson.

London took a deep breath and let it out slowly through his nose. "I have no right to wear this badge any longer."

Dusty looked as though he were going to be sick. "Matthew, this is downright ridiculous! You're not makin' sense."

"No? Listen, there are two reasons why I can't wear this badge. First, I violated my oath by turning two killers loose to save Amy's life. Second, there's a roaring monster inside me known as revenge that I am going to satisfy by personally hunting down Hale Van Horn. I'm going to kill him with my bare hands. A bullet is too good for him, and so is a rope. He's going to suffer while I kill him an inch at a time. Revenge and the badge don't go together, and I'm going to have my revenge."

Anderson lifted his hat and ran his fingers through his thinning hair. "Matt, no one in this town holds it against you for turning Barth and Hale loose in order to save Amy's life. I haven't heard one such word from anybody."

Pulling off his badge and holding it in his hand, London said, "I appreciate that. But even if I could get past number one, nobody is talking me out of number two. I'm going to have the pleasure of beating the life out of Hale Van Horn. No arrest, no judge, no jury."

Will Baker shook his head. "It won't happen that way, Matt. I know you too well. That kind of killer isn't in your soul. I believe you *can* go after Hale and bring him in for trial."

Tears moistened Matt London's brown eyes. Without comment he placed the badge in Baker's hand and said solemnly, "You are sheriff now, Will. The posse hasn't been able to find the Van Horns, but I *will* find them. I promise to bring Holly back when I return." With that, he walked out of the office, closing the door behind him.

The ex-sheriff decided to visit all the farms in the area again, starting with the Van Horn spread. Something was not adding up right. The Van Horns were holing up somewhere near, and somebody had to have seen them. People could not move about without being seen.

As he rode across the windswept, snow-covered plains, London's mind filled with memories of Amy. He wept openly as he rode his horse across the land, the frigid air freezing the tears on his cheeks. Then he felt the burning hatred for Hale Van Horn surface once again. "I'll find you, Hale," he said through gritted teeth. "And when I do, you'll pay!"

On his way to the Van Horn farm London stopped at every house he came to. At each one the former sheriff heard the same story: No one had seen any sign of the Van Horn gang, nor of the two women they had taken with them.

At the Bryant place London was offered a cup of coffee and a chance to thaw his bones before riding on. The Bryants had not attended the funeral, and London had briefly wondered why before realizing they were not up to braving the cold. They offered their sincere condolences on his terrible loss.

He told the Bryants he was going to ride to the Van Horn place and check it out again. Some of the houses were built with underground hiding places during the Indian wars, and he speculated that the Van Horn house might have one. The Van Horn family might be hiding right there on their own place.

Heavyhearted, London left the Bryant farm. The sun was shining brightly but gave no respite from the bitter cold. The breath of man and horse rose in white plumes in the frigid air, adding to the harsh brilliance of endless white.

Yearning for vengeance, London soon reached the perimeter of the Van Horn homestead and rode toward the buildings a quarter of a mile away. The place still looked deserted. But as he drew near the house a rifle shot cracked in the frozen air.

The bullet hummed by London's head, and he dived from the saddle, grabbing his rifle. Another shot echoed across the snow-covered prairie, chewing snow near his feet. London zigzagged his way toward a snow-blanketed woodpile while more shots were fired at him, and as he dropped behind the woodpile one shot was close enough to shower him with snow.

Lying flat, London knew that he had been right: The outlaws had been holed up here all the time. But where had they kept the horses? The animals had not been in the barn when the posse was here a few days before.

More shots plowed into the woodpile. Gripping his rifle, London realized he could be in deep trouble. If all five Van Horns were here, they could easily maneuver him into a cross fire. He cursed himself for letting his hatred for Hale Van Horn keep him from thinking straight. He should have approached the place from its blind side.

All he could do now was fight back. It would be impossible to make it to his horse. Bullets whined past him as he pushed away snow and rearranged some of the wood, fashioning a crude gunport. Easing himself into a firing position, he sent several shots toward the house. Within a few minutes he had determined from the shots returned at him that there were only two men firing at him, and they were both in the house. He fired a couple more shots into the open windows where the two men were positioned.

Suddenly only one man was shooting. This meant either that he had hit one of his assailants or that the other man was outside now, working his way among the outbuildings so as to get him locked in a cross fire.

London studied the layout as best he could from his position. The house was almost straight in front of him. A short distance to the left of the house was the privy, and a toolshed sat some thirty feet to the right. Close to it was a wagon shed. Set back slightly from the shed was a large barn.

More shots came from the man in the house. He was now using a revolver. London fired back several more times before the hammer made a hollow click on an empty chamber. Keeping his eyes riveted on the window, he whipped out his revolver. At that moment the man changed position and exposed his bulky form, and London sent in two quick shots. He heard a cry of pain, and the shadowed figure straightened up, clutching his neck. He hovered for a moment before toppling through the open window, hanging over the sill. It was Barth Van Horn.

Abruptly a barrage of pistol shots came at London from behind the toolshed. London caught sight of his assailant's hat and face as he returned fire and the man ducked back. The face was only a blur; the man had moved too fast. It had to be one of the Van Horn brothers, but which one? Amy London's widower hoped it was Hale.

The man darted between the toolshed and the wagon shed, and his heart skipped a beat. It *was* Hale. A ferocious gleam lit up Matt London's dark eyes, and his lips curled in an animallike snarl. Glorious anticipation welled up in the ex-sheriff as he realized that he would indeed have his revenge. This was Hale Van Horn's day to die!

It was apparent to London that Hale was working his way behind the wagon shed to the huge barn. The sheriff opened fire on the edge of the wagon shed where he expected Hale to appear, but the outlaw surprised him by suddenly shooting from the opposite side. Nevertheless, London's shots kept Hale pinned in place.

Both men reloaded several times, and whenever there was a lull, London poised himself to try again. He sent three more shots from behind the woodpile before he heard the hammer of his gun strike an empty chamber.

London's gloved fingers ran around his cartridge belt, finding only empty loops. He was out of ammunition.

The outlaw must have figured out that the sheriff's gun was empty, for he took that opportunity to run to the barn, plunging inside. Matt London swore when he saw his chance to hit the villain slip by him.

Quickly he thought of Barth Van Horn and the gun he had been using. Weaving his way across the yard, he headed for the window where the body was draped over the sill. Several shots followed him from the barn, but the buildings in between gave him protection. Holstering his own gun, London picked up Van Horn's revolver from where it had fallen from the dead man's hand. In the cylinder was a single unspent cartridge. Van Horn was not wearing a gun belt.

London thought about his situation and reaffirmed that he did not want to use a bullet to kill Hale. The murderer was going to die at London's bare hands. He would try to make Hale use up all his ammunition and then go in and get his hands on him.

Dashing between buildings, London drew more fire from Hale and was forced to use his remaining bullet to cover himself. Then suddenly the shooting stopped and everything fell silent. Hiding behind the wagon shed, London took off his hat and pushed it past the corner. Even this drew no fire. Hale apparently had run out of ammunition too.

Dropping Barth Van Horn's revolver in the snow, he shouted, "What's the matter, Hale? You out of bullets?"

"Why don't you come in and find out?" challenged the big man.

"I'll do just that!" Matt London's blood was on fire with the vivid memory of Hale Van Horn's lighting the fuse cold-bloodedly on Amy's trembling body. His veins throbbed. He wanted to crush, to destroy the Dutchman.

London's fury had not overridden his good sense, however. He knew that Hale might still be armed. Standing by the open door of the wagon shed, he noticed a large gunnysack stuffed with straw lying in a corner. He stepped inside, grabbed it, and then moved to the corner of the shed. He studied the barn for a long moment. The wide door was closed, and the wall boards were tight—no cracks or knotholes through which Hale could watch him approach the barn.

London set out. As he crossed the snow toward the door Hale's booming voice rang out again. "What you waitin' for, London? Come and get me!"

London eased along the barn wall until he was next to the door, which was slightly open, though less than an inch. Holding the fat gunnysack in one hand, he took hold of the door handle with the other. In one smooth move he swung open the door and flung the sack inside.

The sound of heavy footsteps came from inside, followed by a loud grunt. Hale had been waiting with a pitchfork, London figured, and had taken the bait, burying the tines of the fork in the gunnysack before he realized what had happened.

Matt London charged in, slamming his full weight against Hale, who was surprised and off balance. The two men bounded across the floor and crashed into the chest-high wall of the horse stall.

Getting to their feet, they locked in a hand-to-hand struggle. Hale attempted to use his weight advantage to throw London to the floor, but the ferocity of London's wrath made him unshakable. London slammed Hale into the wall savagely, momentarily stunning him. But when the big man regained his senses, he swung a meaty fist, connecting with London's jaw. The pain of it served only to rouse the tall lawman to incredible fury, and he quickly peppered the Dutchman with a violent series of punches, whipping the man's ponderous head right and left.

Hale tried to grasp his opponent in hope of clamping him in a bear hug, but London seized his wrist, pivoted, and threw him over his shoulder. With a loud thud Hale hit the floor, the wind gusting from his lungs. London was on him in a flash. Straddling the outlaw, he punched his face unmercifully with savage blows. Hale sagged, gasping for breath, but London rolled him over, sank his fingers in his hair, and began pounding his face against the frozen earthen floor.

"You killed my wife!" hissed London. "For that I'm going to spread your brains all over this barn!"

London pounded Hale's head hard against the floor again and again and again. The man was unconscious, and blood was flowing from his nose and mouth, but London kept on pounding. Suddenly he stopped and looked down at Hale.

It was as if he had suddenly awakened from a bad dream. He blinked, drawing deep breaths, and then relaxed. Gone was the desire to kill this man. He shook his head and stood up. It was as if Amy's voice was calling to him, telling him that if he went through with it, he was no different from Hale Van Horn.

In that decisive moment as he stood over the battered, unconscious killer, he realized that there was something else—something other than the memory of Amy—that would not let him finish what he had sworn he would do. It was the lawman in him. From somewhere in his innermost being came the realization that the law he had served as sheriff of Yellowstone County was not just an abstract concept. It was an integral part of him. The badge that he had worn as a lawman was vital to his life.

London went to his horse and took a pair of handcuffs from the saddlebags. When he returned to the barn, Hale Van Horn was starting to come around. London cuffed the semiconscious man to an upright post, and then he made a thorough search of the house and outbuildings. He found no secret hiding places; the Van Horns must have been holing up somewhere else. He also determined that all weapons and ammunition had been removed from the premises.

London found Barth and Hale Van Horn's horses tied behind the house. He stripped the saddles and bridles from them and put them into stalls, making sure that the two animals had plenty of hay. He would send someone from the town livery back for them later.

Finishing that chore, he went to check on Hale and found the big man conscious but groggy. He released Hale from the post and stood him up, handcuffing the killer's hands in front of him.

The bloodied man batted his eyes and shook his head. "What're you doin'?" he asked, slurring the words like a drunken man.

Pulling a lariat from a wooden peg on the wall of the barn, London replied, "It'll be easier for you to walk in the snow, as deep as it is, with your hands in front of you."

"*Walk?*" said the outlaw, widening his foggy eyes. "There's no need to make me walk to town. I've got a horse—two horses, countin' Pa's."

London made a slipknot with the lariat and dropped it over Hale's shoulders, cinching it tight around his waist. "True. But they look *real* tired. It'd be much kinder to let them have their rest. Besides, it's only four miles to town."

"My feet will freeze!" complained Hale.

"I don't really care," London said dully.

"What about Pa's body?"

"Believe me, in this temperature it'll keep. Let's go."

Hale Van Horn walked in front while Matt London trailed behind on his horse, holding the rope that was wrapped around the killer's waist. The snow was over a foot deep and made walking difficult.

Van Horn knew that complaining would do no good. There was a noose waiting for him in Billings, and the man on the horse was going to make sure it went around his neck. He cursed at Matt London's cleverness. If he had been on horseback, Hale might have had some slight hope to escape. This way, all hope was gone.

Chapter Thirteen

Matt London and his prisoner had been moving toward Billings for about an hour. The wind had begun to pick up again, whipping against them, tearing at their heavy coats. The whiskers on London's horse were frozen white spikes.

Hale Van Horn's clothing was packed with snow from the waist down from the many times that he had stumbled and fallen. As he plodded ahead of London's horse, tethered by the rope around his waist, his teeth were constantly chattering and his breathing was ragged, frosting in little clouds above his ice-encrusted mouth.

They forged slowly ahead, with London's thoughts drawn incessantly to memories of Amy. Soon the two men were passing a high bank lined with thick, naked brush and a string of cottonwood trees shining silver-gray in the pale light of the winter sun. Suddenly from the thicket came the report of a revolver.

London felt the bullet lance through his right thigh. There was no pain, just the dull sensation of it passing through flesh. Then the bullet tore into his horse's belly, and the animal gave a grunt, followed by a brief whinny, before it fell beneath its rider.

London vaulted from his saddle, jerking on the rope attached to Hale Van Horn. The big man fell backward just as the bushwhacker fired again. The bullet whined past London's ear.

Thinking fast, London lunged toward Hale, whipping out his empty revolver. As he was scrambling, he caught a glimpse of Jimmy Van Horn. The youth appeared to be alone. Dogging back the hammer, London jammed the muzzle against Hale's head while holding the man's beefy neck in the crook of his free arm. He could feel warm moisture running down into his boot, but as yet there was no pain in his wounded leg.

London shouted, "Come out of there and throw down your gun, Jimmy. If you don't, I'll kill Hale right here and now!"

Hale was about to tell his little brother that the sheriff was out of bullets, but he hesitated. For all he knew, London might have taken some ammunition from Barth Van Horn's gun. He decided not to take the chance. If Jimmy was here, Clete and Ben could not be far. Even if London had a round of shells in his revolver, he could not take on three guns at once. The realization made Hale feel almost relaxed.

"I said come out and throw down your gun, Jimmy," London repeated.

"Forget it, Sheriff," Jimmy answered. "You won't kill my brother. You're a lawman—and a lawman won't shoot a man in cold blood. I'd say it's mighty safe to leave Hale in your care till I get back with Clete and Ben."

"Get back?" Hale interrupted. "You mean you staged this ambush all by yourself, you fool kid?"

"Ben and Clete had to go for supplies to that tradin' post north of here, since they couldn't go back to Billings. And they ain't back yet. You ought to thank me, Hale, instead of givin' me grief," he added belligerently. "When you didn't show, I figured it was better to come out after you myself than to wait around. Besides, this way I can lead Ben and Clete to you and London in no time. The tracks you're makin' are real easy to follow."

Laughing, the youth swung into his saddle, shouting as he rode off, "Don't worry, Hale! We'll be back!"

As the kid galloped away, a cold, sinking feeling settled

in Matt London's stomach. With no horse and a wounded leg he knew the kid was right. He was not going to get far.

Taking the gun from Hale's head, London stood up with difficulty. He looked sadly at his horse lying on its side in the snow. A crimson stream from its midsection was turning the snow bright red. The poor beast was breathing hard.

Hale Van Horn gave his captor a speculative look. "Why don't you shoot the poor critter, London?"

Favoring his wounded leg, London shoved his revolver into its holster and replied crustily, "You know why."

"Just what I thought," sneered Hale, rising to his feet. "You ain't got no bullets left."

Matt London wanted to examine the wound in his thigh but did not want to get jumped while he was doing it. In a gritty, threatening tone he said, "Sit down, Hale."

The big man bristled, as if thinking he had the advantage. London could not hide the stream of blood soaking his pantleg. Seeing the hint of rebellion that flashed in Hale's eyes, London pulled his empty revolver and growled, "I can't use it to shoot you, mister, but I can use it to cave in your skull. After what you did to my wife, it wouldn't take much to give me an excuse to do so."

Hale studied the tall lawman with hostile eyes. But the hostility was mixed with respect. Slowly he eased himself down on the ice-crusted snow.

After tying the outlaw securely to a tree to keep him from getting the upper hand, Matt London sat down and inspected his wound. The slug had torn through his thigh about an inch from the back of his leg. It was starting to throb terribly. He pinched down tight around the wound; blood oozed from between his gloved fingers, staining the snow. He pulled off his belt and cinched it around his thigh as a tourniquet. Again he was acutely aware of the moisture inside his boot. He figured that it was between two and three miles to Billings, and there was no way he could walk that far on his bleeding leg. Lifting his eyes, he looked around, getting his bearings.

Studying the white landscape, London remembered an old log cabin nearby. It sat in a shallow valley about a half-mile off the main road to Billings—about a quarter-mile from where he stood.

His horse gave a final whinny and breathed its last. London was jolted by the hatred searing through his body. The Van Horns had killed his wife; they had killed his horse. Now they would have the satisfaction of killing him too.

Pinning the outlaw with a steely look, he snapped, "All right, Van Horn. On your feet. And don't think about doing anything stupid. My conscience wouldn't bother me at all if I were to leave you tied up somewhere. Without moving around to keep your blood flowing, you wouldn't last very long in the cold."

Keeping the restrained killer in front of him, Matt London limped through the snow toward the abandoned cabin. From time to time he stopped to loosen the leather tourniquet for a few minutes. Each time he did so, a crimson spot was left on the snow. The icy wind was whipping across the prairie, but the snow that had fallen had crusted over, and it was not blowing much at all. As if the footprints were not enough, London was leaving a bloody trail, simple for the Van Horn brothers to follow.

As they trudged through the snow Hale Van Horn smiled to himself. He had figured out where they were heading and thought cynically how considerate it was for London to provide a more comfortable place to wait for Jimmy, Ben, and Clete to come for him. He grinned in anticipation of what was ahead. He did not want his brothers to have the pleasure of killing London; he wanted that for himself. Sheriff Matthew London was doomed. Once they had made it to the cabin, Hale would jump the wounded man and kill him.

The sun was past its apex in the cold Montana sky when Matt London and his prisoner reached the log cabin. London looked around the one-room structure, relieved to find it intact. The windows were dirty and frosted with ice; the low roof was held up by three four-by-four posts sunk into the dirt floor; and other than a small charred remnant in the dusty stone fireplace, the only supply of wood was a rickety chair and a small oak table.

Closing the door against the cruel wind, London limped over to the fireplace. He found some old newspapers in the dust in a corner. With difficulty he painfully bent down and picked them up.

Shaking the dust from the papers, London looked at his prisoner. "Since you and your brothers smoke, Hale, you must be carrying some matches."

The outlaw nodded, unbuttoning his coat with his shackled hands. "Yeah, I got some."

"We'll burn the chair first," said London. "Then the table."

He was unprepared for the sudden, ferocious kick to his thigh that Hale gave him. London dropped to the floor with pain shooting like knives up and down his leg. Nausea swept over him when Hale's heavy boot lashed out again, connecting with his face. He rolled on the floor, grimacing and sucking air through his teeth, his body jerking in a spasm of agony. The whole room seemed to be whirling around him.

The hulking outlaw laughed wickedly as he stepped in and kicked his enemy's wounded thigh once more. Then he knelt behind London and swung his shackled hands over his captor's head, pulling the chain of the handcuffs tight against his throat. "Now, lawman," he hissed, "you die!"

The short chain pressed savagely against London's Adam's apple, cutting off his air. Although his right leg felt as if it were on fire and his entire body was racked with spasms of pain, London knew that somehow he had to break the big man's hold or he would soon be dead. Thinking fast, he reached back and jabbed his thumbs violently into Hale's eyes.

The outlaw screamed and released London. He swayed on his feet, howling in pain and rubbing his eyes, trying to clear his vision.

London stood up and whirled about. The picture of Hale Van Horn lighting the fuse on Amy's trussed-up body flashed before him, and blazing fury ignited a fresh determination to come out of this battle as the victor. In desperation, knowing that what he was about to do would lance more pain into his wounded leg, London clenched his right fist, threw all of his weight behind it, and drove a brutal blow to Hale's jaw. It sounded like an ax hitting a tree. The huge man was lifted off his feet and sent flying across the room.

Hale landed flat on his back and stayed there, out cold. Staggering, London dropped to his knees. He swayed for a moment and then fell forward onto his hands. He shook his head, trying to dislodge the mist that tenaciously clung to his brain.

He stayed in that position until the room quit spinning. Then he got up and limped to his prisoner, sliding up Hale's eyelids for assurance that the man was completely unconscious.

London dragged the limp body of Hale Van Horn to the middle of the room. Pulling the key from his pocket, he unlocked the handcuffs and cuffed the prisoner's hands around the center post of the cabin. Then taking the matches from Hale's pocket, he started a fire in the fireplace, using the old newspaper and the pieces of the chair. As the welcome flames crackled he took off his gloves and held his numb hands near them. The heat felt good. After a few seconds he tended his wounded leg, loosening and then retightening the tourniquet.

Within five minutes London was feeling warmer. He unbuttoned his sheepskin coat and opened it toward the fire, wanting to soak up all the heat he could before the wood was gone. The pieces of the chair were old and bone-dry, and they were burning up quickly.

The raw wind howled through the chinks in the walls and the door of the log cabin. The chair pieces had provided little more than fifteen minutes of fuel. London limped over to the small table and ripped off the legs, carefully laying them on the fire. He eyed the tabletop and figured that when he put it in the fireplace, it would provide an additional hour of warmth.

Standing at the frost-lined window, London peered out over the windswept Montana plains, waiting. Reliving the last three weeks, his mind settled on Amy. With her gone, he had little to live for anyway. He pictured her again, standing on the porch, looking so beautiful in her bright red robe, her long black hair flowing in the cold dawn breeze. London closed his tear-dimmed eyes and whispered, "Oh, Amy! Why did you have to die? I love you, Amy! I love you!"

Two hours passed. The fire had burned out a half hour before, and the cabin was freezing cold. Hale had continually been slipping in and out of consciousness, causing London to wonder if he had punched him hard enough to give him a brain concussion.

The relentless wind whipped against the cabin. London limped about, working his arms. His shivering gradually intensified until his joints rattled and his teeth chattered violently. There was only one good thing about the bitter cold: It had caused his leg wound nearly to stop bleeding. His strength however was ebbing. His ears, nose, and lips were without feeling.

He hobbled over to the wall and slid to the floor, thinking that for all the good it was doing, his thick sheepskin coat might as well be paper. He figured he would freeze to death within another three hours—but that would be preferable to the kind of death the Van Horns had planned for him.

He found himself getting sleepy, and though his chance of survival against the Van Horn brothers was nil, his need to hold on to life as long as possible drove him to his feet, and again he began pacing.

The pain in London's leg increased as he walked on it, but he forced himself to keep moving. Soon, however, his energy was spent, and he staggered to the window and peered once again through the frosty glass. Blinking, he squinted and watched intently. He thought he saw movement, but he could not see clearly through the dirty window. He had to be sure. Limping to the door, he stepped out. There were three black dots coming across the snow-mantled prairie.

His heart quickened pace. Jimmy had found his brothers. They were coming to rescue Hale and to kill Matt London.

London hurried back inside and closed the door. He had never felt so helpless in all his life. He had absolutely no way to defend himself. Faltering, he made it to the farthest corner of the room and sat on the cold floor. All he could do now was wait for death to come in the form of three venomous killers.

Soon the sound of snow crunching under horses' hooves reached London's ears, then the muted sound of voices above the whine of the wind. A moment later the face of Ben Van Horn appeared at the window.

Ben looked at the limp figure of Matt London slumped against the wall. Then he grinned and disappeared. A few seconds later the door burst open, and Ben and Clete entered the cabin, guns drawn.

London looked up at them with dull eyes, unable to offer any resistance. "What took you so long?" he said sarcastically.

Holding his gun on the ex-sheriff, Ben said, "We were havin' us a little fun at the tradin' post, if you must know, London. But it ain't nothin' compared with the fun we're gonna have with you now. Get his gun, Clete. I'm gonna check on Hale."

Clete yanked London's gun from its holster, and then he asked over his shoulder, "How is he?"

"He's alive," came Ben's level reply. "Been beat up pretty bad. Almost frozen. We've got to get him on his feet." Calling through the open door, he shouted, "Jimmy! Come in here!"

By the time Jimmy appeared, Ben had found the keys to the handcuffs in London's pocket. He helped Hale to his feet, holding his brother's arm around his shoulder. Ben said, "Here, Jimmy, take hold of him like this, kid. Walk him around till I tell you to stop."

Ben then turned his attention to the half-frozen man sitting against the wall. An evil expression was on Ben's face as he said with menace in his voice, "Clete, let's have us that fun now."

Dragging London outside into the icy wind, they unwound a rope hanging from the pommel of Ben's saddle and cut off two short lengths. After tying a loop at one end of each rope, they bound London's wrists to the other ends and hoisted him up, throwing the loops over the protruding ends of the roof beams. When the loops were securely in place, Ben stepped back and laughed fiendishly into London's face as the wounded man hung there a foot off the ground. "Mister Sheriff, you are gonna die hard!"

Clete gave a hoarse laugh. "Yeah. *Real* hard!"

Then the brothers went back into the cabin to see how Hale was doing.

Matt London hung limply against the ropes that held him, his face colorless. The cruel wind lashed his hair, the frigid air painful to his lungs. He rather welcomed the cold; he was almost completely numb, making it easier to face his inevitable torture and death.

Ben, Clete, and Jimmy emerged from the cabin, and Ben laughed truculently. "Okay, Jimmy, you shoot him first. Now, don't kill him, boy. Just hit him in a leg or one of his hands. We'll take turns cuttin' him into a piece of bloody meat. I'll decide when he gets a bullet through the head."

Jimmy argued that one of his older brothers should shoot the sheriff first, but Ben lashed back, telling the youth to obey him.

While they were wrangling, Matt London hazily saw two riders approaching from behind the Van Horn brothers, backlit by the setting sun. He could not tell who the riders were.

Jimmy finally agreed to fire first. He eared back the hammer of his revolver and took aim at the lawman's right hand. London had braced himself for the new pain, but the gun bucked, and the slug chewed into the wall of the cabin, missing by an inch. Ben and Clete laughed, making fun of their little brother's poor marksmanship.

With their full attention on Jimmy the older brothers were still unaware of the approaching riders. But London had focused on them now, and he saw them dismounting fifty feet behind the Van Horns. His pulse quickened. In spite of his faltering vision he could make out the forms of two women. One was a blonde, the other a brunette.

Holly and Sandra!

Ben, Clete, and Jimmy, intent on their mission, were laughing loudly. Ben drew a bead on Matt London's hand. Snapping back the hammer, he sneered as he said to his younger brother, "Now I'll show you how it's done, kid."

London's head began to swim. Hanging by the ropes had been more than his bruised, bleeding, half-frozen body could endure. He fought the gray cloud that was descending over his consciousness, but it was too powerful. His eyes rolling back in his head, he passed out.

With his revolver aimed straight at London's left hand, Ben shouted angrily, "Hey, Sheriff! Don't you pass out on me! I want you to feel this!"

Suddenly Holly's voice cut through the air like a whip. "Drop the gun, Ben!"

The three brothers' heads snapped around, and their jaws sagged. Jimmy gasped, while Clete's eyes bulged as he stared at his sister. Holly stood poised, her feet spread apart, each hand holding a cocked Colt .45. The muzzles were trained on Ben, who eyed his blond-haired sister with utter fury.

Holly's voice was as icy as the air when she repeated, "Drop the gun, Ben!"

Ben's mouth was a tight line as he kept his gun pointed at London's hand and snarled at Jimmy, "You said you tied 'em up good, kid. Can't you do anything right?"

Jimmy did not answer. He let his gun hand hang loosely at his side.

Clete threw a murderous look at the brunette standing behind Holly before gazing back at the two threatening muzzles. His own gun was still holstered.

Holly held her guns steadily on Ben, circling around to his right. Again she barked, "Drop that gun, Ben!"

Ben Van Horn clenched his teeth and slowly moved his aim from Matt London's hand to his heart. "London has to die, Holly."

A fierce light shone in Holly's pale blue eyes. "Get rid of the gun, Ben, or so help me I'll kill you!"

Ben laughed, his gun still trained on the unconscious man's heart. "Who do you think you're kiddin', baby sister? You'd never shoot down your own kin!"

Clete chuckled hollowly. "He's right, Holly, and we all know it. You wouldn't shoot your own brother."

Jimmy emitted a weak laugh, as though attempting to appear as confident as his older brothers.

Holding the ominous black revolvers steady, Holly blared, "So help me, Ben, if you pull that trigger, I'll drop you in your tracks." Glaring at the other two, she added, "Clete, Jimmy, throw your guns on the ground."

"Don't do it!" shouted Ben. To Holly he rasped, "If you're gonna shoot me, girl, you'd better get it done. Because I'm about to drill the sheriff, and then all three of us are gonna kill *you*!" Pointing with his head at the other woman, he added, "And we'll kill her too."

Watching Holly from the corner of his eye, Ben flexed

his hand on the gun, preparing to squeeze the trigger. Clete and Jimmy braced themselves.

Nervously, Holly licked her lips. She saw Jimmy raise his gun and Clete's hand move slowly toward his. The spunky blonde knew she was deadly accurate with the cocked guns in her hands, and she could spit death at all three brothers and kill them in less than three seconds. But she was doing battle with Ben's words: *You'd never shoot down your own kin!*

Holly's throat tightened when Ben gave her a sly grin and started to press the trigger. She felt every muscle in her body tense. The flesh crawled along her spine. The wind gusting around the eaves of the old cabin sounded to her like the wailing of a lost soul.

Six shots roared in a rapid staccato, thundering like cannons as their echoes rebounded off the cabin walls. The Van Horn brothers, hit by two bullets each, dropped to the snow as if a rug had been jerked out from under their feet. All three were instantly dead.

But Holly had not pulled the triggers.

She spun around. Chief War Horse, Leaning Tree, and four Crow braves were standing at the far corner of the cabin, holding smoking rifles. Swallowing hard, her face blanching white, Holly gasped and lowered her guns.

As the brunette dashed past Holly toward the unconscious sheriff, the Crow chief looked at the blonde with his dark, impassive eyes and said, "War Horse not think you could shoot brothers. It had to be done."

Holly nodded silently, holstering her guns.

Then War Horse spoke to his four braves. "Help women take Matt London inside."

The Crows untied the sheriff and carried the unconscious man into the cabin, wrapping him in one of their colorful blankets and laying him on the floor. War Horse explained to the women that when Lone Bear had ridden back to their village and told what happened at the hanging, the chief and his braves set off to find the Van Horn brothers and capture them. They had intended to honor their agreement with London and bring the men back to Billings for trial.

The iron shoes making it easy to distinguish white men's horses from Indians', War Horse and his men had tracked Clete and Ben to the trading post. The Indians had kept themselves at a distance, well hidden, following the brothers back to the cabin with Jimmy. There they had waited, just out of sight. If London had had the situation well in hand, they would have followed the lawman at a discreet distance back to town, ready to provide assistance if necessary. But when they had arrived at the cabin and had seen that Matt London was in trouble, they had decided to make their move. They had been about to do so when the two women rode up.

Holly checked Hale. He was alive but in a stupor. She found the handcuffs and, pulling her oldest brother's hands behind his back, fastened them to his wrists. She returned to the Indians and said, "Chief War Horse, we deeply appreciate you and your men coming to our rescue. My brothers were bad men. Very bad. But I don't think I could have shot them. If you hadn't done it, Ben would have killed Sheriff London."

War Horse accepted Holly's words of appreciation stoically.

"Would you and your braves mind waiting outside while we try to revive the sheriff?" Holly then asked him.

The chief allowed a thin smile and silently motioned his men out, then closed the door.

Matt London sensed himself returning to the cold world. Someone was rubbing his hands briskly. Two soft, feminine voices floated above him. His mind felt like a bird in flight, circling low and about to land.

The dizziness was ebbing. Slowly his eyes fluttered open. He could make out two fuzzy figures hovering over him. One was a brunette, the other a blonde.

Suddenly London remembered the scene just before he

had passed out. *Holly and Sandra! Somehow they have rescued me!*

"He's coming around," London heard one of the voices say. It was a familiar voice. The sound of it picked at the back of his mind. It was not Holly's voice. Nor was it Sandra's.

Wait a minute! he said to himself. *I must be delirious.* He blinked hard, trying to clear his vision. *The blonde is Holly. But the brunette . . . the brunette is—* No! *It can't be!*

Chapter Fourteen

"**H**ello, darling," said Amy, smiling.

As Matt London's vision cleared he matched the beautiful face to the familiar voice. He was struck dumb. His mouth was clamped shut, and his tongue was glued to the roof of his mouth. He could only stare, with his heart slamming his ribs violently.

"You're going to be all right, darling," Amy said softly. "Your leg isn't bleeding anymore. We'll get you back into town to Doc Alton."

London found the strength to sit up, and tears welled in his eyes. As Amy also began to weep he cupped his wife's face in his hands. Abruptly his tongue loosened, and his jaw relaxed enough for him to speak. "You're alive!" he whispered. "Amy darling, you're alive! But how—?"

"I'll explain in a moment. But right now, just hold me."

Holly Van Horn looked on, tears streaming down her own face as Matt and Amy London wept in each other's arms. No one seemed to notice the cold.

When emotions had settled somewhat, Amy and Holly explained what had happened the morning that Barth and Hale Van Horn had escaped. As soon as London and his deputy had left the London house and were out of sight, the three Van Horn brothers had tricked Dusty Canfield into unlocking the door and had knocked him out.

Though the three women had struggled, they had been easily subdued by the men. Ben and Clete, furious at

179

Sandra for testifying against the Van Horns, decided to use her to force London into releasing Barth and Hale. They made Sandra put on Amy's bright red robe, saying that from a distance London would think it was Amy. Ben was sure that with the sheriff believing his wife was wrapped in dynamite, he would back down and release the two prisoners. And Sandra, Ben and Clete agreed, deserved a good scare. Ben had not dreamed that Hale would be so viciously angry at Sandra that he would actually set off the dynamite.

Holly explained that her brothers had taken over the Bryant farmhouse when they first had deserted their own place. Each time the lawmen and the posses came, the Van Horns and their captives were hidden in the safety cellar under the Bryant house, from where everything that was said in the house could be heard. The Bryants had been under the threat of death to cover for them.

London now understood why the Bryants had not attended the funeral.

Holding her husband tight, Amy told him that before he had arrived at the Bryant place that morning, Ben and Clete had already ridden to the trading post. When Hale and his father had heard London tell the Bryants he was going to the Van Horn farm, the two men decided to take a shortcut and beat him there, just as soon as the sheriff rode away. That left Jimmy to guard Amy, Holly, and the Bryants.

When a couple of hours had passed and Hale and Barth had not returned, Jimmy got nervous. He tied everybody up and left to check it out. The prisoners soon freed themselves after he left. Amy and Holly took two of George Bryant's horses and headed for the Van Horn place, where they expected to find London, Jimmy, Hale, and Barth Van Horn. Meanwhile the Bryants planned to head for town in their wagon to get Will Baker.

When the two women arrived at the Van Horn place, they found Barth Van Horn's body. Hale and Jimmy were gone, and there was no sign of Matt London. Holly, despite the shock of seeing her father's dead body, had the presence of mind to take her revolvers from where she had kept them hidden in the house. Then she and Amy set out to find Matt London, following the same tracks in the snow that Jimmy had followed earlier.

London knew the rest. Jimmy had tried to ambush him and rescue Hale, but the attempt had failed, leaving the youngest Van Horn to go in search of Ben and Clete. After Jimmy had found his brothers, either at the trading post or on their way back from it, the three of them had tracked London and Hale to the cabin.

Holly explained to London all that had happened at the cabin after he had passed out. When she added that the Indians were still waiting outside to make sure he was all right, London smiled and said, "Good. That means War Horse is not angry with me for releasing Barth and Hale in order to save you—I mean, Sandra, God rest her soul."

With Amy's and Holly's help Matt London rose to his feet and checked on Hale, who was still dazed. "Hale, old boy," London said bitterly, "you're all alone now. There'll be nobody to break you out this time. You're going to the gallows."

London invited Chief War Horse and his braves into the cabin. He was thanking them for their help when Leaning Tree pointed at the window. Outside a wagon was approaching, accompanied by a man on horseback.

Within moments the Bryants reined in their horses, and Alice Bryant shouted, "Is everything all right, Holly? Our wagon broke a wheel just as we were setting out to get Will. We got here as soon as we could."

Will Baker leaped from his saddle and took the woman he loved into his arms. Then he stared incredulously at Amy and said with a wide smile, "I was so happy when the Bryants told me you were still alive!"

The beautiful brunette held her husband's hand tightly. "Thank you, Will," she said softly.

Looking into Holly's eyes, the deputy said, "Honey, I'm so sorry for all this tragedy you've had to endure. And poor Sandra. To have met such a horrible end when she was trying to see justice done." He hugged the young woman to him. "Thank heavens you're all right."

Alice Bryant looked at Matt London with a pinched face and said, "Sheriff, I feel just awful that we couldn't tell you Amy was alive. The Van Horns would have killed us all."

"I understand, ma'am," London assured her. "There was nothing else you could do."

The Crows carried Hale Van Horn out to the wagon. The Bryants had brought along several blankets, and the outlaw was wrapped in two of them. Hale said nothing. His face was immobile, sullen, as if he was wondering why they were bothering to save his life when he was going to hang.

Matt London leaned against the wagon and kept one arm around his wife. His deputy, holding Holly by the hand, said to him, "Matt, Hale looks like somebody pushed his face into a threshing machine. Were you the one who beat him up?"

"Well, I had to work him over a little bit to capture him," London said. "I was out of ammunition."

"You could have killed him with your bare hands, couldn't you?"

London nodded and answered quietly, "Yeah. Guess I could've."

"But you didn't." Baker grinned. "You were going to bring him in for trial, weren't you?"

"Yeah," London replied, not quite meeting the deputy's gaze.

"Didn't I tell you that's the way it would be?"

London looked at Amy, then at Baker. "Yes, you did."

Pointing to the badge that was pinned to the outside of his coat, Baker said, "You notice I'm still wearing my deputy's badge?"

London did not answer, but his brows were raised in question.

From his pocket Will produced the sheriff's badge that

London had given him, and he held it out. "After you rode off, the townspeople got word that you had turned in your badge. There was a big meeting. None of them blame you for what you did. It was unanimously agreed to hold the job open for you, when you returned." Still extending the badge, Baker said, "Well?"

London smiled broadly and accepted it, pinning the badge on his coat.

Amy stood on her tiptoes and kissed him. "Let's go home, darling."

The bodies of the Van Horn brothers were placed in the cabin, where they would keep until the undertaker came for them.

War Horse gripped London's hand in the white man's style. "Matt London, my people admire and trust you. We Crow cast no blame on you for what you did to save squaw."

"Thank you, War Horse." London grinned.

Leaning Tree and the other Crows also wished London well, and then they rode off with their chief.

After tying the spare horses to the back of the wagon, Holly Van Horn and Will Baker mounted up double on his horse with the blond woman in front. Cuddling her close to him, the deputy said, "Holly, I can't wait another minute. I have a question to ask you."

"What is it?" she queried, snuggling even closer.

"I would like to provide you a permanent home . . . as Mrs. William Baker. Will you marry me?"

Twisting around to look into his eyes, the young woman replied in a serious tone, "I'll have to think it over, Will."

Looking a little surprised, the deputy bobbed his head. "For how long?"

Laughing and throwing her arms around his neck, she said, "For about two seconds. The answer is *yes!*"

The Bryants and the Londons cheered, congratulating the newly engaged couple. Then they all climbed up into the wide wagon seat, where they sat four abreast. London and Amy snuggled together under a blanket, clinging to each other as the wagon rolled toward Billings in the deepening purple of the winter sunset.

Pulling his horse close to the wagon, Baker said, "Say, Matt, are you still holding the wager money on my bet with Dusty?"

"Sure am."

"Do you consider marriage as valid as courting?"

Laughing, London replied, "Even more so."

"Good," replied the deputy. "When we get to town, I'll let you give me the money right in front of the old geezer."

Holly looked back over her shoulder and asked, "Will, what's this wager business all about?"

Snickering, Baker said, "Honey, I'll let Dusty tell you all about it when we get to town."

The arctic wind howled like a banshee over the vast Montana prairie, but its mournful voice had no effect on Matthew London. He could not have been happier. He had his prisoner in shackles, his badge on his chest, and his wife in his arms. As far as he was concerned, it might as well have been spring.

THE BADGE

BOOK SIX
SHOWDOWN
by Bill Reno

Sheriff Clint Wilson is known far and wide for his firm hand and his fast draw, and he has always managed to live up to his reputation. His success is partly due to his wife, Sarah, and their teenage children, Mike and Melanie, since their home provides the sheriff with a refuge from the dangerous world of an Oklahoma law enforcer in the 1880s. But when Jed Bratton and his gang brutally beat Sarah and the children, savagely violating his wife and daughter, the center of Wilson's life comes apart. When Melanie dies from the incident, revenge consumes the lawman.

Intent on finding the Bratton gang and seeing that justice is done, Wilson sets out to track them. He doesn't know that his son follows after him, however, against his father's wishes. The tragic events that occur as a consequence unhinge the lawman, and he turns to the bottle for solace.

With his family ties dissolving, Wilson is dealt another blow when his badge is taken from him because of his drinking. But even that does not cause the lawman to change his habit. Only the love of a woman and the threat of losing her brings the sheriff around—and just in time to prepare for the most challenging showdown of his life.

Read **SHOWDOWN**, on sale August 1988 wherever Bantam paperbacks are sold.